Drowning t

A Heavenly Highland Inn Cozy Mystery

Cindy Bell

Copyright © 2013 Cindy Bell

All rights reserved.

All rights reserved. No part of this publication may be reproduced or transmitted in any form or by any means, electronic or mechanical, including photocopy, recording, or any information storage or retrieval system, without permission in writing from the publisher.

This is a work of fiction. The characters, incidents and locations portrayed in this book and the names herein are fictitious. Any similarity to or identification with the locations, names, characters or history of any person, product or entity is entirely coincidental and unintentional.

All trademarks and brands referred to in this book are for illustrative purposes only, are the property of their respective owners and not affiliated with this publication in any way. Any trademarks are being used without permission, and the publication of the trademark is not authorized by, associated with or sponsored by the trademark owner.

ISBN-13: 978-1497318922

ISBN-10: 1497318920

More Cozy Mysteries by Cindy Bell

Heavenly Highland Inn Cozy Mystery Series

Murdering the Roses

Dead in the Daisies

Killing the Carnations

Bekki the Beautician Cozy Mystery Series

Hairspray and Homicide

A Dyed Blonde and a Dead Body

Mascara and Murder

Pageant and Poison

Conditioner and a Corpse

Makeup, Mistletoe and Murder

Hairpin, Hair Dryer and Homicide

Blush, a Bride and Body

Table of Contents

Chapter One 1

Chapter Two 22

Chapter Three 35

Chapter Four 49

Chapter Five 66

Chapter Six 80

Chapter Seven 103

Chapter Eight 128

Chapter One

Vicky closed her eyes and drew a deep breath of the fresh summer air. It filled her lungs in a soothing way that allowed her mind to ease. The front parking lot of the Heavenly Highland Inn stretched out before her, sloping upward slightly along a hill. Beyond it to the right was the lush, manicured lawn that led to the gardens. To the left was a path that wound around behind the inn to the pool and the nearby woods. There was a sense of peace brought on by the quiet tweets of birds and the distant calls of squirrels. When paired with the flawless, blue sky above her, Vicky found it impossible not to feel content.

Vicky tried not to think of the night before. It was supposed to be a romantic evening to celebrate a six month anniversary. She and Deputy Sheriff Mitchell Slate had been dating for that long, which she didn't realize until he announced it. Vicky wasn't one for anniversaries. She also didn't enjoy putting labels on relationships. She was a free spirit and though she cared deeply for Mitchell she hadn't expected the turn their conversation had taken.

Mitchell wanted to discuss their future, as if it was a step by step plan they could follow. Of course it made sense that Mitchell would think this way. He was very logical, always following the evidence in a crime and rarely led by emotion. When Vicky had responded that she didn't think they needed to put a timeline on things, and preferred to let things flow as they did, his reaction had been startling. Instead of quietly nodding as he usually would, Mitchell had insisted that they needed to discuss some kind of commitment.

"I'm invested in this," he said as he met her eyes. "I want to know that you are, too."

"It's not a business opportunity," Vicky had pointed out with annoyance.

"So, you're saying you don't see a future for us?" Mitchell had responded with growing irritation. "Just be honest with me about it, don't string me along."

"Don't put words in my mouth," Vicky had countered as she stood up from her chair. "I love you, Mitchell, I've told you that, if that's not commitment enough then I don't know what you want from me."

"I want to know that you want this to last," Mitchell replied as he also stood up. The delicious meal that Vicky had spread out on the table between them was forgotten. Their voices rose within the confines of the large apartment that she lived in within the inn. "Is that so much to ask?"

"Maybe it is," Vicky pushed back, startled by the anger in her tone. "What's next, you're going to want me to sign a contract?"

"What?" Mitchell snapped. "You're being ridiculous."

"Am I?" she asked as she marched towards the door of the apartment. "Well, I certainly can't understand why you would want a future with a ridiculous person," she opened the door and held it for him.

Mitchell stared at her with a mixture of hurt and confusion. He opened his mouth to speak, but instead he walked right past her. When Vicky closed the door behind him her mind was reeling with emotions. She and Mitchell had never fought like that before. But after a few weeks of him dropping hints about wanting to move their relationship forward, Vicky's nerves were on edge. She didn't like to feel pressured into anything. It was crushing to think about how she had spoken to him. She hadn't been able to sleep a minute as she regretted kicking him out of the apartment.

Mitchell was the first man she had ever imagined a future with, and she wondered if she wasn't pushing him away because it frightened her. But as she looked out over the clear, blue sky she forced herself not to think about it. Instead she tried to focus on the family reunion that was taking place at the Heavenly Highland Inn. She was planning the event of course, and was looking forward to immersing herself in her work to avoid the troubles that were weighing on her mind. The Carter family was very well off and quite large, so they had booked several rooms in the inn.

"What's wrong, Vicky?" Aunt Ida asked as she walked out of the lobby of the inn and onto the white, Roman-style porch. "It looks like someone strangled your cat."

Vicky arched an eyebrow at her aunt's words. "I don't have a cat," she pointed out with some confusion.

"It's just a saying," Aunt Ida rolled her eyes as she rested her elbows on the railing beside her niece. Aunt Ida had become like a mother figure to both Vicky and her older sister, Sarah, after their parents were killed in a car accident. Though Aunt Ida had her quirks and insisted she was in her thirties when sixties would be more accurate, she was always there for her nieces when they needed her. She also lived at the inn, as she had when Vicky's parents owned it. She stayed in one of the guest rooms.

After their parents' death Sarah and Vicky had taken over the inn. Sarah was responsible for managing it, while Vicky coordinated events as well as other aspects of the day to day running. The inn was a very sought after destination, especially by the wealthy and elite. It was a grand old inn with lots of character and top class facilities. It was located in a beautiful setting surrounded by gardens and mountains and had hosted some big name guests over the years.

"Just spill," Aunt Ida insisted and locked eyes with Vicky who was leaning against the front pillar of the porch.

"I'm just waiting for the Carter family to arrive," Vicky insisted with a mild shrug. "They're going to be here for the weekend for a family reunion," she explained hoping to steer Aunt Ida away from the topic of her demeanor.

"Mmhm," Aunt Ida nodded slowly. "And that's got you so glum?" she asked with disbelief.

"I'm not glum," Vicky protested and averted her gaze from her aunt's. Aunt Ida had a knack for seeing right through her.

"Is it Mitchell?" Aunt Ida asked, though the certainty in her voice made it clear she already knew that it was. Vicky cast a glance at her aunt with wide eyes. There were times that she could be so perceptive that Vicky questioned whether she might be just a little psychic.

"It's Mitchell," Vicky admitted with a sigh as she began to pace back and forth across the porch. She didn't want to appear riled up when the Carters arrived.

"What did he do?" Aunt Ida asked, and Vicky smiled with relief that her aunt didn't instantly take Mitchell's side. Mitchell was amazing at his job and was always available to help them with anything they needed. He was from the deep south and was a very kind and respectful man. Aunt Ida had never hidden the fact that she thought he was downright handsome and a great catch.

"It's not something he did," Vicky frowned as she met her aunt's eyes. "We just have different desires in life."

"Oh?" Aunt Ida asked as she leaned against the railing of the porch. "What desires might those be?"

"You know, the usual things," Vicky shrugged as if it was no big deal, but it was clear in the creases of her features that it bothered her. She cared very deeply for Mitchell. "The whole picket fence and babies scenario."

"Oh, I see," Aunt Ida patted her niece's arm gently. "I know from my own experiences that men don't always understand a woman who doesn't count down the minutes to a ring and a mini-van."

Vicky smiled at that. Aunt Ida was a perfect example of a woman who had what some might classify as less traditional desires in life. She had traveled the world, never slowing down long enough to marry though she had had plenty of lovers. She had no desire to have children of her own, but had doted on her nieces and spoiled them with exotic gifts and experiences. Vicky had always looked up to her way of life, and though she adored her mother, she had always found Aunt Ida to be much more interesting.

Her older sister, Sarah, on the other hand had been eager to marry, and was swift to begin having children. Vicky admired her, too, and she couldn't argue the point that Sarah was blissfully happy with her family. Vicky just hadn't decided for herself what she wanted, and in fact she had been doing her best to avoid the decision for quite some time.

"It's not so much that I will never want that," Vicky admitted thoughtfully. "But I certainly don't want it now."

"Well, did he propose to you?" Aunt Ida asked curiously.

"No," Vicky shook her head. "Nothing like that."

"Then what?" Aunt Ida pressed as her eyes narrowed slightly. She was very protective of her nieces and would get a little aggressive with anyone that might cause them the slightest harm.

"He just wanted to talk about our future together," Vicky shrugged mildly.

"That's all?" Aunt Ida asked as she studied her niece. "What's wrong with that?"

"Nothing really," Vicky admitted with a frown. "I just don't see a need to talk about it."

Aunt Ida paused for a moment and tapped her fingertips lightly on the railing of the porch. "You know, Vicky, sometimes men can feel insecure, too. Maybe he just wants to know that you do want a future with him. I mean, if you do. You don't have to define what that future might be, but maybe he's thinking you're just biding time with him."

"That couldn't be further from the truth," Vicky sighed and closed her eyes. "I know that I overreacted, but I just don't like to feel pressured."

"Life is pressure, sweetie," Aunt Ida patted her arm again. "But it's a lot easier to deal with when you have someone you love to share it with."

Vicky nodded solemnly as her aunt's words sunk in. She was a little embarrassed by how quickly she had blown up over a simple request from Mitchell, but she wasn't ready to admit to that yet. Luckily, before she would have to admit to it, a town car pulled into the large parking lot and rolled up to the front steps of the porch. A driver stepped out and walked around to the passenger door closest to the porch. He opened the door, and a man stepped out. Lawrence Carter was exactly as Vicky expected him to be. She had never met the man before, but knew that he came from old wealth, and he had a good reputation in the community. She was honored when they had chosen to have their family reunion at the inn.

Now that he was standing on her front porch she was a little nervous. He had the presence of an aristocrat, and the arrogant glare to back it up. His gray hair was balding and had retreated to the middle of his head. When combined with his steel blue eyes, it made him appear to be a very powerful man. He was fit, with broad shoulders and a hint of muscles beneath his polo shirt. He looked uncomfortable in his jeans, and Vicky assumed he was used to wearing trousers instead. He probably didn't take vacations too often.

"Are we the first to arrive?" he asked before even greeting her.

"Yes, you are," Vicky smiled warmly as a woman ascended the porch steps behind him. She had long, brown hair that glistened in the sunlight. It was clear that she was at least twenty years younger than her husband. Vicky assumed she was not the first Mrs. Carter. Behind her was the driver of their town car, carrying four suitcases.

"Would you like some help with that?" Vicky offered as the man struggled up the steps.

"He can handle it," Lawrence said dismissively. "Can we just get signed in?"

"Absolutely," Vicky smiled again and led them into the inn. She stepped behind the desk and pulled out a small clipboard. On it she had printed all of the names of the Carter family and any guests they would be bringing. She checked off Lawrence and Alina Carter, and then turned to the computer.

"We've got you set up in a suite," she explained as she retrieved the keys from the lockbox behind the desk. "I can take you up now so you can get settled in if you like, or I could give you a tour of the inn," she suggested.

"We'd like to get settled in," Alina nodded quickly.

"You go ahead, I'm going to wait here for Max and the boys," Lawrence replied. Vicky presumed he was referring to his two adult sons, Mike and Simon, and his brother, Max.

"Don't worry, Lawrence they'll be here," Alina said with a smirk. "You haven't run them off, yet."

"I know they'll be here," Lawrence replied in a short tone. "I just want to be here to greet them when they arrive."

Vicky quietly observed the exchange before interjecting. "Well, Mrs. Carter we can just take the elevator over here," she smiled at the woman as she led her and the driver with all the suitcases to the elevator. As the doors slid shut Alina let out a loud sigh of relief.

"He's been so impossible. He's so sure that something is going to go wrong this weekend. I can't say I don't agree with him," she laughed mildly. "Does anything ever go right at a family reunion?"

Vicky nodded at her words. "It can be tough. But hopefully you will all get to enjoy a very relaxing weekend. If there's anything I can do to help you with that, don't hesitate to ask."

"Thank you," Alina said as the elevator doors opened and Vicky led her towards the suite. "But as long as you have plenty of booze, I'm sure everything will be just fine," she laughed at that, but it was more bitter than amused. Vicky was glad she had restocked the bar and even ordered extra just in case. Vicky smiled again as she pressed the key into Alina's hand.

"Like I said, anything at all, just let me know."

"Thanks again," Alina smiled, and Vicky noticed a shadow in her pale blue eyes. It seemed to Vicky that perhaps Alina was not as content to be part of the reunion as her husband might think.

As Vicky rode the elevator back down to the lobby she glanced at her watch. Sarah was taking a little time off to spend with her family. Vicky knew that she would be calling any minute to check in on the reunion and find out how Vicky was handling everything.

When the elevator doors opened Vicky was greeted by a gathering of Carters in the lobby.

She spotted Lawrence in the middle of the gathering. Two younger men were standing near him. From their similar looks Vicky assumed that the men were Lawrence's sons. One was older, perhaps in his thirties, while the other appeared to be in his twenties.

Beside Lawrence was a man who looked to be about his age and had similar strong features but a full head of dark hair. He had his arm around the shoulders of a woman slightly younger than him who had pretty round features and a kind smile. Vicky assumed this was Lawrence's brother, Max, and his wife, Connie. Beside Mike was another woman who appeared to be in her thirties. She had a long, floral print dress on, a head of loose red curls, and a nervous smile. Vicky guessed this was Mike's wife, Charlene.

The front door swung open and two more women with husbands in tow walked into the lobby. Though they had softer features they shared the same regal arrogance that the rest of the Carters did. Vicky easily guessed that they were Beverly and Sasha, Max's daughters. That meant that everyone should have arrived.

Everyone seemed to be mingling fine until a young woman, probably the youngest of the group in her early twenties, stepped up beside Simon and slid her arm through his. She had straight black hair, a short skirt, and a tight blouse. She was gorgeous from head to toe, in the way that no one could overlook. But most of the women present seemed to be less than impressed with her presence. This had to be Simon's fiancée, Jane.

"Oh, I see you brought her," Mike said gruffly as he glanced over at Jane. Jane shifted uncomfortably and lowered her eyes. Her cheeks flushed and it was clear that she was insulted by the comment.

"Yes, of course I brought my fiancée," Simon snapped in return as he locked eyes with his brother. Vicky realized she had stepped right into the middle of a hornet's nest. Luckily, Alina stepped off the elevator at that moment and distracted Mike from Jane.

"I have everyone's room keys available," Vicky said brightly hoping to ease the tension of the situation.

"Good," Simon said as he glanced at her. "I'll take ours," he held out his hand for the key.

"Sure just let me get it out of the lockbox," Vicky said quickly and walked over to the desk. As she tapped a few keys on the computer to log into the system and check out the keys she was just about to hand out, Mike's wife, Charlene, began gushing.

"I know that this is our first official family reunion," she said quickly. "And I'm just so proud to be a Carter, so I brought something special for everyone," she glanced shyly at Mike. He nodded encouragingly to her. She pulled a box out from behind her suitcase and opened it up.

"I had these made for this weekend," she explained as she began pulling out baseball caps from the box. Each one had a bright blue "C" imprinted on it.

"Ha, just like my necklace," Lawrence chuckled as he displayed a circular, gold pendant with a raised 'C' on the front of it.

"How lovely, Charlene," Alina said, though her tone was dripping with sugar. Beverly and Sasha were quick to take a few of the hats and hand two over to their husbands.

"This was a great idea," Beverly said in a friendly tone. "It's a souvenir that we can keep to remember the weekend."

"Thanks, Charlene," Simon said as Mike slipped on his cap, and Simon reached into the box. He pulled out the last cap.

"Oh," Charlene said quietly as she shifted uncomfortably. "Mike had said that Jane wouldn't be coming this weekend, so…"

"It doesn't matter, she's not a Carter yet," Mike pointed out and offered Jane a cruel smirk.

Simon smiled at his fiancée who was struggling not to let the insults get to her.

"She will be soon enough," he murmured as he settled the cap onto her head. "You look beautiful, Mrs. Carter," he leaned in and kissed her softly in front of the whole crew. Vicky had to hide a smile in reaction to Simon's defense of his fiancée and the ripple of annoyance it sent through the rest of his family. She was certain that this reunion was going to be much more interesting than she had anticipated.

"Here you are," she said as she began handing out the keys. "Once you get settled in you're welcome to explore, I have lunch scheduled to be served beside the pool in an hour."

"Sounds perfect," Lawrence said as he smiled at Alina and pulled her close. "Maybe you can give me the tour of the suite."

"Gladly," Alina replied with a purr.

"Ugh," Mike and Simon both groaned and glanced away from their father. Lawrence tugged his baseball cap further down on his head and winked lightly at Charlene and Jane.

After all the guests had headed off to their rooms Vicky headed to the kitchen to check on the progress of the lunch they would be serving. She also sent a text to Sarah letting her know the Carters had arrived and everything was going smoothly besides the fact that there was plenty of drama going on between family members.

Sarah texted in return that she had to check it out and would be there in time to help with lunch. Vicky smiled a little as she knew that no matter how much Sarah enjoyed being with her family she couldn't stand to stay away from the inn for too long.

Chapter Two

As Vicky set the tables up beside the pool she thought about what Aunt Ida had said to her. She was setting up little vases filled with daffodils and was lost in her thoughts when Sarah came walking up behind her.

"This looks great," Sarah smiled as she admired the tables and the cheery décor that Vicky had chosen to make the occasion seem all the more festive.

"Thanks," Vicky said with a smile. "I'm glad you approve."

"I'm not checking up on you," Sarah promised with a laugh. "I just wanted to see all this drama you were talking about."

"Oh, you could cut the tension with a knife," Vicky assured her. "Seems like most, if not the entire Carter clan, is not so fond of the youngest son's choice of fiancée."

"Oh boy," Sarah chuckled and shook her head. "You know I'll never understand people approving or disapproving of someone else's relationship. I mean you can't control who you fall in love with."

"That's for sure," Vicky agreed. Before she met Mitchell she might not have agreed with her sister, but he had certainly swept her off her feet. The idea of love took on a whole different meaning with him. It was strange, and wonderful. "And the two do seem to be in love," Vicky added. "I hope it all works out for them."

"Me, too," Sarah agreed. "Speaking of love," she coughed sharply.

"Nice," Vicky winked at her sister and then turned away to set out a few more napkins.

"You never tell me what's going on with you and Mitchell," Sarah pouted a little. "I tell you all about my romance."

"That's because it's nothing but romance," Vicky pointed out. "Well, romance and peanut butter and jelly sandwiches."

"You'd be surprised how romantic a good PB and J can b..."

"Okay, I don't want to know," Vicky laughed and shook her head again. She really did admire her sister's relationship with her husband who was always very supportive of her and their family. "The truth is Mitchell and I are still trying to work a few things out."

"What's to work out?" Sarah pressed. "He's gorgeous."

"That's true," Vicky grinned.

"And so very charming," Aunt Ida added as she stepped out onto the pool deck. She was wearing a loose flowing skirt. This was a little unusual for Aunt Ida as she was very fashionable and preferred to wear clothes that fitted her figure snugly.

"Hi, Aunt Ida," Sarah smiled as she leaned in to kiss her aunt on the cheek. "I was just trying to pry a little dish out of this one."

"Good luck," Aunt Ida rolled her eyes. "I'm glad you're both here."

"Why?" Vicky asked suspiciously as she set up the last wine glass on the table.

"Well, you know girls, I have something to show you," Aunt Ida grinned as she looked from Sarah to Vicky and back again. Vicky braced herself and tried to hide an amused smile. Anything Aunt Ida was this excited about was bound to be pretty interesting. Aunt Ida placed her foot on the chair beside her and hiked up her long, pale yellow skirt.

"What is that?" Sarah gasped when she caught sight of the bright red rose wrapped around Aunt Ida's ankle. The skin was still crimson as if the tattoo was fresh.

"Do you like it?" Ida asked as she smiled at her nieces.

"Uh," Sarah stammered, her eyes wide. The tattoo was well done, but it was surprising to see one on her aunt's ankle and leg.

"It's beautiful," Vicky said quickly, though even she was more than a little shocked. Of all the crazy antics that Aunt Ida could get up to, Vicky never expected her to get a tattoo. Even she didn't have any tattoos.

"Why?" Sarah asked as she began to recover from her surprise. "Why did you get a tattoo?" she looked at Aunt Ida as if she was a rebellious teenager that had sneaked out in the middle of the night.

"Oh, I don't know," Aunt Ida sighed, though her lips were curved into a gleeful smile. "I was feeling a little bored. Not much spice in my life," she frowned at that and then smiled admiringly at her tattoo. "I met this amazing man, his name was Stone, or Rock, it could have even been Pebble, I don't really remember. Anyway, he kept going on and on about how beautiful my ankle was, and that it needed to be accentuated," she purred the word, drawing it out in a seductive tone.

"With a rose?" Sarah asked with disbelief. "Didn't it hurt?"

"Well, with a tattoo," Ida admitted. "He suggested something a little more dangerous, like a snake or a skull, but I told him absolutely not. I told him I wanted something delicate and pretty, so he suggested a daffodil, I think because he is Welsh and they are the national flower of Wales. But, after thinking about it I decided on a rose because it is one my favorite flowers," she smiled. "Yes it did hurt, but not too bad. The whole time he told me stories about the tattoos on his body, and by the time he was done, I was smitten. With the tattoo I mean," she added quickly. "Pebble on the other hand, I decided was just a little too artsy for me."

"It's very pretty," Vicky volunteered and earned a dirty look from Sarah. "What?" she asked as she looked at her sister. "Are we not going to talk about that four leaf clover on your…"

"Vicky!" Sarah growled in warning. Aunt Ida laughed and covered up the rose with her skirt again.

"Don't worry girls it's just a tattoo. It's not like I got a piercing."

"Were you considering a piercing?" Sarah asked with wide eyes. "Aunt Ida, they can lead to infections and..."

"Come along, Sarah," Aunt Ida giggled as she led her away from the pool. "I'd like to see that four leaf clover of yours."

Sarah shot a glare over her shoulder at Vicky who smiled innocently before turning back to the tables. One of the waiters who worked in the restaurant attached to the inn came out with a few platters of snacks for the guests to dine on while they waited for their lunch. As if smelling the food, Mike Carter suddenly appeared.

"Oh, that looks great, I'm starving," he moaned as he settled into one of the empty chairs.

"Enjoy," Vicky smiled as she filled his glass with wine. Soon the entire Carter clan was joining each other at the tables.

Even though it had seemed as if they might try to tear each other apart earlier, Simon and Mike seemed to fall into easy banter, exchanging memories of their childhood with their cousins. The spouses looked on with amusement. Alina and Lawrence continually asked for refills of their wine glasses and everyone seemed generally relaxed and glad to be together. Vicky was relieved that the lunch had gone much better than she expected. She stepped back into the inn to grab another bottle of wine and noticed that Jane followed after her.

"Do you need something?" Vicky asked kindly.

"No, I think I just need to rest a little bit," she admitted. "It was a long drive and I'm not used to so much wine," she added. Vicky smiled at her with compassion.

"If you need something to settle your stomach..." she began to offer, but Jane waved her hand dismissively.

"Oh no, thank you, I'll be fine," she promised as she walked towards the elevator. Vicky watched to make sure she got to the elevator okay and then continued to the kitchen to retrieve the wine. By the time she returned with it the mood had taken a decided change for the worse. In fact Mike was nearly up out of his chair as he leaned across the table towards Simon.

"You don't even care what kind of filth you're bringing into this family," he accused, his voice rising higher with every word. Vicky froze at the edge of the pool and watched as Simon locked eyes with his older brother.

"Jane is an amazing woman, I don't understand why you have such a problem with her. When you married Charlene we all welcomed her into the family with open arms," he pointed out. "The same with Beverly and Sasha's husbands."

"That's because none of them was a gold-digging con-artist," Mike hissed back.

"Careful Mike," Simon smirked as he studied him. "Your jealousy is showing."

"What's that supposed to mean?" Charlene asked with an embarrassed blush.

"It doesn't mean anything," Alina assured the woman and glowered at the two brothers. "Why don't you just settle down and let your father enjoy this weekend."

"Oh, I don't mind," Lawrence chuckled as he watched his sons squabble. "It reminds me of when they were just boys fighting over a toy."

"Mike isn't fighting over Jane," Charlene snapped and now her cheeks were flushed with anger.

"I have more wine," Vicky said bravely as she walked up to the tables.

"I believe we may have had enough," Alina replied icily. "I'm going upstairs."

"I'll be right there," Lawrence called out. "As for you two," he turned to his sons. "There's plenty to do here, give each other some space."

"Gladly," Mike growled as he stood up from the table and tossed his napkin down dramatically. He stalked off across the manicured lawn. Charlene, Beverly, and Sasha, along with their husbands decided to take a walk in the gardens. When Vicky walked away with a stack of dirty plates and glasses, Lawrence and Simon were the only ones still at the table.

"I just don't get it, Dad," she heard Simon saying. "Jane is wonderful, she's beautiful, she's smart. What does everyone have against her?"

"She's not of our class, son," Lawrence replied in a serious tone. Vicky closed the door behind her as she didn't want to hear the rest of that particular conversation.

***

After giving Lawrence and Simon plenty of time to have their discussion about the worthiness of different classes, Vicky glanced outside to see that they had left the tables. She stepped out of the lobby and followed the path towards the pool. There were still a few wine glasses and dirty plates to be cleaned up. Normally the waiter would do this, but Vicky didn't mind the task, and had sent him home early.

There were a few beer bottles scattered around on the benches and a bit of water splashed up on the pool deck. She wondered if perhaps Lawrence and Simon had gone for a swim. She began gathering the bottles as she walked around the edge of the pool. As she tossed them in a nearby trash can, she felt a strange sensation. She could tell that something was simply wrong. It was as if the lapping of the water was slightly off. Reluctantly she shifted her gaze towards the pool. That was when she saw the body floating face down in it.

Chapter Three

"Aunt Ida!" Vicky screamed out as she shed her shoes. "Call an ambulance!" she shouted as she dove into the pool.

Aunt Ida poked her head out the door just in time to see Vicky splash through the surface of the pool. Vicky pushed the body upward and rolled the man over in the water. His face was slightly bloated and blue. It was clear that he was not alive, but she still felt as if she should try to save him just in case there was any life left. By now her shouting had drawn the attention of others, including the man who had just arrived to service the pool. He gasped as he saw her struggling with the body. He helped Vicky tug the body out of the pool and laid him on the pool deck.

"What happened?" he asked as Vicky attempted to give the man CPR. He had no pulse, and he was not breathing. Vicky knew he was already gone. It took her a moment because of the distortion of his features but she soon recognized him as Simon, Lawrence Carter's youngest son.

"Oh no," she sighed as she sat back on her heels and stared down at the body before her. The ambulance along with its blaring sirens pulled into the parking lot of the inn. A moment later the EMTs were attempting to revive Simon.

"He's already gone," one said to the other. Vicky nodded in agreement and wondered how she would ever notify the family. When an ambulance is called for an emergency the police are automatically contacted as well, so Vicky was not surprised when Mitchell came jogging around the side of the inn. He paused to speak to the EMTs and then began to approach her. She looked up at him with a frown. She knew that he was likely still upset with her, but he was exactly who she had been hoping to see.

"Are you okay?" he asked her, though his tone was slightly clipped.

"I am," Vicky sighed as she stood up and shook her head. "I can't believe this happened."

"How did it happen?" Mitchell asked as he pulled out his notebook. "Just so I can fill out my report," he added and avoided eye contact. His sandy brown hair shimmered in the sunlight. Vicky tried not to notice.

"Well, they were all drinking heavily after lunch," Vicky frowned as the water dripped off her. "He must have slipped, or maybe even passed out and landed in the water."

"Do you have an idea of how long he was in there?" Mitchell pressed. Vicky glanced up at him and wished she could lean on him for a little comfort. She knew that if she did he wouldn't turn her away, but she wasn't ready to yet.

"I'm not sure," Vicky admitted. "The last time I checked on the group was about two hours ago and Simon and his father, Lawrence, were out here by the pool."

"Okay, I'll put that in my report. Looks like this will be considered an accident, but it's best to have our bases covered," he tucked the notebook back into his pocket. "Do you need anything else?" he asked and attempted to meet her eyes.

"No," Vicky sighed as a new sense of reluctance washed over her. "I had better change into dry clothes and then I imagine I'll be warding off questions from the guests."

"Okay, let me know if you need anything," he offered, his eyes softening with sympathy.

"Thank you," Vicky said with genuine gratitude.

Vicky took a deep breath as she headed back into the inn. It made her heart ache to think that the family's reunion was going to be permanently marred by the tragic loss of a family member. After quickly changing into dry clothes she went back to the lobby. Sarah was waiting for her there as she had rushed back to the lobby as soon as Vicky let her know there was an emergency at the pool.

"Is it true?" Sarah asked as she met Vicky's eyes. She had talked to the EMTs in the parking lot as they returned to the ambulance without a patient. The coroner would take possession of the body.

"I'm afraid so," Vicky frowned and leaned against the wall just inside the lobby. "The family doesn't know yet."

"It will be okay," Sarah said gently and squeezed her sister's shoulder to offer her some support. Vicky was so grateful she was there. Just as they were walking past the elevator the elevator doors slid open to reveal Jane, Alina, and Lawrence.

"What were all those sirens about?" Alina asked, her eyes wide as she stepped out of the elevator. Jane was standing on the other side of her, Vicky's eyes immediately went to her. All she could think of was how Jane would not have the opportunity to marry the man she loved. She wished that she wasn't the one that would have to tell them.

"I'm sorry to tell you this but there's been a terrible accident," Vicky said as she looked from Jane to Lawrence whose face was shifting from an expression of surprise to one of apprehension.

"What terrible accident?" he asked gruffly. "What are you talking about?"

Sarah stepped in as she rested her hand lightly on Vicky's arm. "It seems that Simon fell into the pool," Sarah explained calmly. "I'm so very sorry, but he didn't make it."

"What do you mean he didn't make it?" Jane cried out. Lawrence grabbed onto Alina for support.

"Wait, what are you saying?" he asked, his cheeks flushed with emotion. "He was fine when I left him there, he said he was just going to finish the glass of wine you poured him," he said as looked at Vicky. Just then the door to the lobby opened from the garden.

"Hello?" Mike called out as he stepped into the lobby. "What's going on here? Why is there an ambulance and police?"

"It's Simon," Jane gasped out as she looked up at Mike with tears flowing down her cheeks. "He drowned in the pool."

"Drowned?" Mike stammered as he accepted Jane into his arms. "What are you talking about? Simon can swim!"

"Nobody can swim when they're that drunk," Alina muttered rather callously.

"Alina," Lawrence said reproachfully.

"Well, it's true," Alina huffed as she shook her head. "He probably passed out drunk and fell in the pool. That's why it's an accident, right Vicky?" she asked as she met Vicky's eyes. "I mean, a grown man doesn't just drown without a reason."

Vicky shifted uncomfortably and cleared her throat. "Well, that is the theory," she admitted as she glanced from Alina to Lawrence. "If he had passed out he probably didn't experience any pain," she offered, hoping to reassure him. She couldn't imagine the pain of a father losing his son.

"No way," Jane shook her head sharply. "Simon would never get that drunk."

Lawrence was silent for a long moment before he nodded slowly. "He was drinking much more than usual, I..." he closed his eyes and grimaced. "I knew this weekend was a mistake. We never should have gone through with it."

"No one could have known," Alina murmured and seemed a little dazed as she held tightly to her husband. "No one could have known."

Vicky stayed with them until they decided to return to their rooms. Vicky offered them a full refund if they decided to end their stay at the inn early.

"I just want to see him," Jane said with a shaking voice. "I don't think I'll be able to believe it without seeing him."

"Okay," Vicky nodded and wrapped an arm loosely around her shoulders. She knew that the rest of the Carters were not exactly kind to her. "I'll call someone to drive you, okay?"

"Yes," Jane sniffled as Vicky led her into the waiting area of the lobby where there were a few plush couches.

Once Jane was settled on a couch, Vicky glanced back up at the rest of the family in time to see Lawrence arguing sharply with Mike. Vicky couldn't catch what they were saying, but she didn't find it too surprising. Perhaps they were debating whether they should have stopped Simon from drinking so much.

A few minutes later a cab arrived to drive Jane to the morgue. Vicky thought about joining her, but she wasn't sure if that would be overstepping, and she still had to manage the inn as Sarah had already gone home to return to her family. Vicky sighed as she watched Jane descend the steps on the porch. Just hours before she had been looking forward to spending the weekend organizing the reunion, now she wondered if she would be capable of helping the Carter family with their unexpected loss.

***

The inn was fairly quiet for the rest of the day. There were only a few other guests that were staying that weekend. One out-of-state couple who had chosen the inn to celebrate their honeymoon, and Vicky had not heard a peep from them since they checked in. Another guest, Wilbur Arbor, was a regular at the inn and usually didn't need too much attention.

In fact, Vicky didn't see anyone until Aunt Ida returned from a nap in her room. The excitement of finding the body had exhausted her, she claimed. But Vicky knew better. She had probably run off to text all of her friends in the murder-mystery book club she had recently begun hosting. She had a knack for solving crimes, and often pulled Vicky right into the middle of it. But this wasn't a murder mystery. This was an accident, one that Vicky couldn't help feeling partially responsible for. Maybe if she hadn't brought out that extra bottle of wine, maybe if she had asked them to move along before they were all so drunk, then Simon would still be alive.

Vicky knew it wasn't her responsibility, but she couldn't help but feel a little guilty. If she hadn't been so bent on not having to hear about Jane not being of the right 'class' she might have discovered Simon earlier and been able to save him. There were so many possibilities. When she locked up the inn for the night she took a moment to look out over the pool. In the moonlight it looked so beautiful, it was hard to believe that something so horrible had happened there today.

When she stepped into her apartment she felt the emptiness of it. She always lived alone, however, whenever she came home for the night there was always the potential of inviting Mitchell over. She liked that idea, that knowing that she didn't have to be alone if she didn't want to be. But she also valued her alone time. She took a long, hot shower to try to wash away the events of the day, slipped into some soft pajamas and climbed into bed.

As Vicky lay there she thought about Mitchell, what her life would be like without him. In a split-second Jane's life had been forever changed. The future that she had counted on had vanished without her having any ability to change it. As a result it made Vicky think about what her future would be like without Mitchell as part of it. She didn't like the idea of it too much. Mitchell was more than just a boyfriend, he was an incredibly good friend to her. He had guided her through more than one difficult occasion and been very patient with her when she felt the need to pull away.

Vicky turned on her side and stared at her cell phone on the bedside table. Her mind raced with thoughts of whether she should call him. She was still thinking about it when her phone began to ring. She knew it was him without having to check. Not many other people would dare to call her so late. As she picked up the phone, still debating as to whether she should answer it, she thought about what it would be like if she had been the one to call, and have him not answer. She answered quickly.

"Mitchell?" she murmured as she lay back against the bed.

"I'm here," he replied and the tension in his voice was thick. "I'm sorry I know I probably shouldn't have called."

"Why not?" Vicky pushed with a sudden sense of desperation. "It was just one fight," she pointed out.

"Was that all it was?" Mitchell asked, and he sounded as nervous as she felt. "I wasn't sure what to think, Vicky. The way you just asked me to leave. You've never done that before."

"I know," Vicky replied quietly. "I let things escalate, and it shouldn't have happened."

"No, it shouldn't have," Mitchell agreed. "But I played a part in that too, I think."

"Maybe you did," Vicky replied in a whisper.

"I still want to know Vicky, nothing has changed," he explained hesitantly. "I just want to know where you stand."

"Just give me some time, Mitchell," Vicky replied as her heart pounded.

"Take as much time as you need," Mitchell replied though his voice had a slight edge to it. "I'll be here," he hung up the phone, and left Vicky staring uneasily at the ceiling.

Chapter Four

Early the next morning Vicky made sure that a full breakfast buffet was available for the Carter family. It didn't surprise her however when no one came down for breakfast. She decided that she would offer to bring the breakfast directly to their rooms. As she was heading for the elevator, Aunt Ida waved to her from across the lobby.

"Vicky, I want to talk to you," she said as she hurried over to her.

"Ride up with me," Vicky suggested. "I just want to check in with the Carters and see if they want some breakfast in their rooms."

"Okay," Aunt Ida agreed as she stepped into the elevator with Vicky. "I have to tell you about this dream I had," she said with increasing urgency.

"Dream?" Vicky asked with a frown as she glanced at her aunt. She failed to see how a dream could be so important.

"Yes, it was you and I and Sarah and we were flying," Aunt Ida explained as the elevator began to move. "It was really very beautiful."

"It sounds beautiful," Vicky agreed, though her brows were creased with confusion. "Is it supposed to mean something?"

"Well, I woke up and I couldn't get back to sleep no matter how hard I tried. So, I took a stroll through the lobby to try to wear myself out. I found Will sitting down there just staring into space."

"Wilbur?" Vicky asked with curiosity. "Was he okay?" she asked as she held the elevator door open for her aunt.

"He looked very upset. So, I sat with him and we talked a bit. He said that he needed to talk to you today," she replied.

"All right, well once I'm through here we'll see if we can find him so we can find out what's going on. More importantly, Aunt Ida please don't wander the inn at night. I know it's your home, but I worry about you," Vicky frowned as she studied her aunt intently.

"Oh sweetie, you don't need to worry about me," Aunt Ida assured her. Vicky walked towards Jane's room. She wanted to make sure that she was okay since she knew the Carters were not very friendly to her.

Aunt Ida was still talking about her black belt and ability to defend herself when Vicky heard a voice she didn't expect. Vicky grabbed Aunt Ida by the elbow and motioned silently for her to stop. She had heard Mike's voice inside the room that she knew was assigned to Jane.

"What are you talking about?" Mike growled loud enough to be heard through the door. "You can't do this Jane, you just can't."

"I think it's time the truth came out," Jane countered, her own voice rising with emotion. "Simon is gone now, why can't we just be honest about it?"

"What do you think this will do to my family?" Mike demanded, his voice growing more aggravated. "Are you really that stupid, Jane? So Simon is dead, that doesn't change anything."

"Why?" Jane asked with desperation. "I don't want to keep lying to everyone."

"It doesn't matter what you want," Mike nearly shouted back. "You'll keep your mouth shut, and you'll keep right on lying. Do you understand me?"

Vicky's eyes widened at the intensity of his response. She felt uncomfortable listening in without interfering, but she was also shocked. From what she heard, it sounded like Mike and Jane had been having an affair. Had Mike been sleeping with his brother's fiancée?

"Please Mike," Jane said with tears in her voice. "Don't be angry with me."

"I'm sorry," Mike replied in a softer tone. "I'm sorry. I didn't expect any of this either. But you need to remember to keep this secret. Understand?"

"I understand," Jane replied shakily. As Vicky heard heavy footsteps approaching the door of the room she whisked Aunt Ida down the hallway and out of sight. Once she was sure that Mike wouldn't spot them, she turned to her aunt.

"Did you hear what I heard?" she asked with wide eyes.

"I sure did," Aunt Ida replied with a cluck of her tongue. "With a family of jackals like that, that poor boy never stood a chance."

"But it looked like an accident, do you really think it might have been murder? If it was, do you think Mike could kill his own brother?" Vicky asked with a slight shake of her head. "I never pegged him for a cold-blooded killer."

"I'm sure Simon never expected that he was sleeping with his fiancée either," Aunt Ida pointed out. "Mike's wife also seems smitten with him," she added.

"Well, no matter what anyone thinks of him, I think Mike just showed us his true colors," Vicky said as she folded her arms across her chest.

"I think Jane did, too," Aunt Ida pointed out.

"Maybe Lawrence is right," Vicky said with disappointment. "Maybe she really is just after the family money. She decided one brother wasn't enough and decided to have a relationship with both to make sure that she would have a life of wealth."

"Maybe," Aunt Ida nodded and then frowned.

Vicky glanced down the hallway to be sure that it was clear. The door to Jane's room was closed and there was no one in the hallway. As she walked with Aunt Ida back to the elevator she sighed. It seemed like the Carter family had more skeletons than she could have anticipated.

***

As soon as Vicky and Aunt Ida returned to the lobby Vicky spotted Wilbur Arbor standing beside the front desk.

"Vicky, could I talk to you for a minute?" Will asked as he leaned heavily on the counter in the lobby. Vicky was eager to look through the camera feed from the pool the day before. She planned on reviewing it anyway for insurance purposes, but now she was very curious. She wondered if the cameras might have caught something more than an accident. As she walked behind the desk, Wilbur kept his gaze on her. Ida paused beside him and offered him a warm smile.

"Sure Will, what is it that you need?" Vicky asked as she managed a smile and looked in his direction. When she saw his expression she knew it would not be anything good.

"I'm sorry to bother you," he said quietly. "But I heard about what happened to that young fellow yesterday, and well, I think I should tell you about something I saw."

"Oh?" Vicky asked and leaned forward on the counter. "What is it Will?"

"Well, I heard some commotion beneath my window. I like to look out over the pool, you know," he smiled.

"I know," Vicky replied as he had a reserved booking on the same room every time he stayed at the inn.

"I heard this commotion and I looked out the window, and I saw these two men. One of them was the young fellow that died yesterday, the other, I could only see the back of his head," he shook his head slightly.

"Well, a lot of the Carters were out by the pool yesterday," Vicky said calmly.

"But they weren't just talking," Will said firmly. "I saw the other man wrap his hands around the young fellow. It looked like he was trying to choke him!"

"Oh," Vicky said, her eyes widening. "Are you sure?" she asked hesitantly. Will wore very thick glasses, and even with those he was known for not having the best vision. "Maybe they were hugging or just playing around?" she suggested.

"No," Will said firmly and looked into Vicky's eyes. "I know what I saw," he stabbed his finger sharply against the counter. "They weren't playing around. I almost called the police. I went to get my phone. But when I came back, I didn't see the men anymore. I didn't see the young fellow in the pool either," he frowned. "So, I just assumed the fight had ended. But when I heard that he was dead, I just knew I had to say something."

"Well, I'm glad you did," Vicky replied with a patient smile. "I'll look into it."

"You'll just look into it?" Will asked with mounting aggravation. "I'm telling you I think I witnessed a murder," Will said more urgently.

"Now Will," Vicky said calmly as she looked at him. "We don't know what you saw..."

"Vicky," Aunt Ida said sharply as she walked up behind Will. "If Will says he saw someone attacking poor Simon, then he saw it."

"I'm sorry Aunt Ida, but we can't be certain," Vicky explained as she frowned. "Even if Will did see someone attacking Simon, we still don't know who it was. That's why I'm looking through what the cameras recorded yesterday to see if there's anything captured on video," she looked back at Will. "Will, I will make sure your information gets passed onto the police. If Mitchell has more questions for you, I'll let you know."

Will huffed a little as he could tell that Vicky wasn't taking him too seriously. Aunt Ida looped her arm through his and patted the back of his hand lightly.

"Don't worry, Will, we'll spend some time together," she suggested. "Have I shown you my new tattoo?" she grinned as she led Will back towards the restaurant.

Vicky cringed and then pulled out her cell phone. She frowned as she looked at the phone. She needed to give Mitchell the information just in case, but she wasn't looking forward to talking with him. Normally it was her favorite thing to do, but things were so tense between them that she felt guilty every time she talked to him.

Before she called Mitchell she decided to check the cameras. When she pulled up the feed on the computer screen she grimaced. The picture was grainy and it was difficult to tell what anything was in the image. Still, she rewound it to the day before in the window of time that she believed Simon's death had taken place. As she did she noticed the two men that Wilbur had witnessed. One of the men was not wearing a hat. He was clearly Simon. The other man was wearing a hat, but his back was to the camera. The man in the cap raised his hands as if he might try to strangle Simon, but instead he just waved them with frustration. From the angle that Wilbur had been looking it was possible that it looked like the man in the cap was strangling Simon.

The man in the cap stalked off across the lawn towards the parking lot. Simon sat down on one of the chairs and opened a beer. He was drinking it when a figure appeared from off screen. He must have been standing directly in front of the camera because the image was very blurred. She caught a glimpse of Simon standing up. Then she saw what could have been a struggle. Then the figure moved away from the camera, and there was no one in view. Vicky guessed that during the time the camera was blocked Simon had been pushed into the pool. There was no sound on the recording so she had no idea if there was a verbal argument or a splash. She rolled it back, and watched it again hoping to discover something about the blurred figure. But there was no way to decipher anything.

The one thing the recording did give was a time stamp of the murder. It happened at exactly four fifteen. With this information she decided to run things by Wilbur again. She would then contact Mitchell and hand over the tapes. She wanted to know if he could recall the time he had seen the fight, and whether he had any idea of who the man in the baseball cap was. She found

Aunt Ida and Wilbur in the restaurant with fresh cups of coffee and bagels.

"Hi, mind if I sit?" Vicky asked as she smiled.

"Please do," Wilbur said and got to his feet while Vicky took her seat, then he sat back down.

"Listen Wilbur, I want to talk to you..." Vicky began, but her phone ringing interrupted her.

"Excuse me," she said to Wilbur and Aunt Ida as Ida replenished their coffee mugs. Aunt Ida nodded as Vicky stepped away from the table.

"Hello?" she said into the phone.

"Hi Vicky, it's Mitchell," he said quietly.

"I know who it is," she replied and found herself smiling without meaning to.

"Listen, I have some information about Simon's death," he paused a moment and sighed before continuing. "It was no accident, Vicky."

"Are you sure?" Vicky asked without much surprise. She had been expecting the call.

"Yes, there was alcohol in his system, but he also had defensive wounds, and he did not die from drowning. He died from a blow to the head, which could have happened if he slipped, but that doesn't explain the defensive wounds."

"Oh no," Vicky sighed and closed her eyes briefly. "I just looked at the cameras that cover the pool, there's not much that's helpful on them," she frowned.

"I'm sorry, Vicky," Mitchell said soberly. "I know it's not what you want to hear. I'm going to be over there in about twenty minutes. This is now a homicide investigation, and," he paused a moment before speaking again. "Sheriff McDonald is coming with me."

"Great," Vicky did her best to cover up a sigh. Sheriff McDonald was not someone that she enjoyed seeing. He was a bit of a bully and was always giving Mitchell a hard time.

"Can you please get all the tapes from the pool cameras together from around the time of the murder so I can look at them," Mitchell requested.

"Of course," Vicky replied with a sigh.

When Vicky hung up the phone she turned back towards Aunt Ida and Will who were still chatting over their cups of coffee.

"Well, Will it looks like your suspicions were right," Vicky said as she studied the man intently. Now it was even more important than ever that he recall exactly what he saw.

"What do you mean?" Will asked with surprise as he looked up at Vicky.

"It turns out that Simon's death wasn't an accident after all," Vicky explained as she paused beside the table they were sitting at. "Mitchell just called to tell me that this is now a homicide investigation."

"Oh no," Aunt Ida gasped and shook her head. "What does that mean?" she paused a moment as she looked towards the nearby elevator.

"Someone here killed him?" she asked as she turned back to Vicky.

"It looks that way," Vicky said with a frown. "I doubt that anyone would have just randomly hurt Simon. It must have been one of his family members."

"Or his fiancée," Aunt Ida pointed out.

"Well, it was a man I saw by the pool," Wilbur said firmly. "Of that much I am certain."

"Mitchell asked me to gather the family members in the lobby so that they're easily available to him when he arrives to question them. Will, I am sure Mitchell will want to talk to you as well, so are you okay to stick around?"

"Of course. Anything I can do to help," Wilbur nodded, though his face had paled. None of them had expected this to really turn out to be a murder. As Vicky walked away from the table she called Sarah to inform her of what was unfolding. Even though she was taking some time off she wanted to be kept apprised of any happenings at the inn. This certainly was a happening.

"Do you know if they have any suspects?" Sarah asked after Vicky filled her in on what was happening.

"I think everyone is a suspect at the moment," Vicky replied with disappointment. But of course, there was one particular person that Vicky suspected the most. The person she believed was having an affair with his brother's fiancée.

Chapter Five

Once all of the Carters and Jane were gathered in the lobby Vicky stood nervously in front of the group. As she looked among the faces staring back at her she knew that one of them was responsible for Simon's death. As likely as it was that it was Mike, she still couldn't rule out anyone else. The way the Carters bickered, there was probably more than one reason why they were angry at each other.

"Why are we here?" Alina asked with annoyance. "Don't you think you should be letting us grieve, not disturbing us?"

"Well, this is now a police matter," Vicky explained as calmly as she could. "And in a few minutes Sheriff McDonald and Deputy Sheriff Slate will be here to speak to each of you."

"What?" Jane asked with surprise. "The sheriff, why?"

"Because," Charlene said as she crossed her arms. "They don't think it was an accident."

Vicky quickly studied the faces around Charlene searching for one that might indicate surprise or fear. Although everyone did react with some level of shock, she didn't notice any one looking obviously guilty.

"It's true," Vicky said quietly. "It looks as if Simon's death was not caused by a slip."

"But he was so drunk," Mike reminded everyone, his eyes narrowed. "Obviously he slipped. I mean, who would want to hurt Simon?"

"Well, I know that there was some arguing going on," Vicky reminded the group before her.

"What are you trying to say, young lady?" Lawrence growled as he stared straight at Vicky. "Are you accusing one of us of having something do with Simon's death?"

"No sir," Vicky said quickly as she realized her mistake. "I was just pointing out that there were some charged emotions yesterday. I didn't mean anything by it."

"I bet," Lawrence scowled and looked away from her. Vicky felt a twang of fear. She didn't want to alienate one of the wealthiest men that had stayed at the inn. It could do great harm to the inn's reputation.

"Hello, everyone," Mitchell said as he walked through the door. Sheriff McDonald stepped in behind him. He fixed the entire group with a suspicious glare while Mitchell spoke politely to the family. "I'm very sorry for your loss," he said with genuine sympathy. "I'll do my best to make this as quick and painless as possible. Because of some evidence that the medical examiner discovered we have reason to believe that Simon met with foul play," he glanced among the faces of the people before him. "So, I'm going to divide you up, and all I need to know from you was where you were between three and five yesterday afternoon," he explained as he pulled out his notebook. "Sheriff McDonald will take some of your statements, we need to confirm your whereabouts at the time of Simon's death."

"And if we refuse?" Jane asked shyly. Her cheeks were flaming red. Sheriff McDonald laid his hand on the butt of his gun and stepped up beside Mitchell, his glare deepening though he remained silent.

"You have the right to refuse," Mitchell admitted as his jaw tensed. "However, that will mean that I will have to name you as a suspect and bring you into the station. I just want all of you to know that this is simply to rule out all of you as suspects. With this information documented we can move onto outside suspects."

"Outside suspects?" Lawrence asked with surprise. "Do you mean you think someone just walked off the street and decided to kill Simon?"

"With all due respect, Mr. Carter, with your wealth and the history of your corporation, I believe that it may be possible that someone harmed your son in order to harm you," he arched a brow slightly as he met Lawrence's eyes.

"I never thought of that," Lawrence said slowly. "I do have a few enemies."

"Well, any information about them will be helpful," Mitchell said quickly. "Let's go ahead and get started. Let's see," he glanced down at his notebook where he had written a list of all the family members. "I'd like to speak with Simon's immediate family, and Sheriff McDonald will be speaking with the spouses. If that's all right with you, sir?" he asked as he glanced over his shoulder at Sheriff McDonald.

Sheriff McDonald nodded without a word and pulled out his notepad. Vicky could tell he was trying to be his usual intimidating self. She glanced over at Mitchell, who seemed to be waiting to share a grimace of annoyance with her at the sheriff's behavior. It was the first time he had even looked in her direction. Vicky studied him for a moment and then returned the grimace. As Sheriff McDonald gathered the spouses together, Jane nervously glanced in the direction of the immediate family.

"Do I even count as a spouse?" she muttered under her breath as she stood beside Vicky.

"Yes, you do," Vicky said as she met Jane's eyes. "Just be honest."

"I can handle the questioning," Sheriff McDonald interrupted gruffly. "I'll take it from here. Can you tell me where you were around four yesterday afternoon?" he asked as Vicky stepped aside.

"Of course I can," Jane replied. "I was with Lawrence," she admitted and lowered her eyes.

"Lawrence?" Sheriff McDonald asked with surprise. "Were you alone with him?"

"Yes," Jane sighed. "I wanted to talk to him about Simon, and convince him that we were really in love, that I wasn't after anyone's money," she frowned.

"And about how long were you with him?" Sheriff McDonald asked.

"About a half hour, I think," Jane said thoughtfully. "Yes, it was about four fifteen when we were together, until about five o'clock."

Sheriff McDonald was surprised by the exactness of the time. "How do you know for sure that was the time?" he asked suspiciously.

"I know because I looked at my watch," Jane snapped in return. "I looked at it when I first met with Lawrence because I wanted to make sure I wasn't away from Simon for too long."

"And you looked at it again when you left Lawrence?" Sheriff McDonald pressed as he jotted down the information.

"Actually no," Jane said thoughtfully. "I saw the time on the alarm clock. We were in Lawrence's suite."

"Oh, I see," Sheriff McDonald said as he glanced over at the group that was talking with Mitchell. "Was Lawrence's wife, Alina, with you?" he asked.

"No, I think she was in the garden," Jane replied with a shake of her head. "I don't know, but since everything happened I can barely keep track of what time of day it is," she glanced down at her watch. She stared at it for a long moment. "That's strange," she mumbled.

"What is?" Vicky asked as she looked at Jane's watch, too.

"That's all I need for now," Sheriff McDonald said as he moved onto Charlene, Mike's wife.

"What time is it?" Jane asked Vicky as she moved closer to her, confusion creeping into her voice.

"It's about twelve," Vicky replied as she peered closer at Jane's watch.

"Huh," Jane frowned and tapped the face of her watch. "It must have stopped. It looks like the bit on the side has broken off," she sighed.

"I'm done here," Sheriff McDonald muttered to Mitchell as he tucked his notebook back into his pocket. "You finish up here, and meet me back at the office," he glanced at his watch and then sternly into Mitchell's eyes. "In no more than a half hour, no catching up with your girlfriend."

Mitchell narrowed his eyes but nodded respectfully. Vicky watched as Sheriff McDonald walked out the door of the inn. She could never quite figure him out. When Mitchell finished up with the last of the Carters and their spouses he met Vicky at the front desk.

"Looks to me like everyone has an alibi," Mitchell said casually though he did not meet her eyes directly. "Everyone, except for Mike. Lawrence claims to have been with Jane, Alina and her nieces were in the garden along with Max and his wife. Mike on the other hand said he went for a walk in the woods."

Vicky remembered the man in the cap walking towards the parking lot and the woods on the camera. Could that have been Mike?

"Well, I have a guest here who witnessed an argument between Simon and a man at the pool.

I already had a look at the camera feeds before they were requested for evidence but wasn't able to tell from them who the man was," she shook her head. "But there's something else," she lowered her voice and he leaned closer to her to listen. "Aunt Ida and I overheard a conversation between Jane and Mike. I think they are having an affair."

"Oh," Mitchell narrowed his eyes and glanced over at Mike who was talking animatedly with Jane. "Well, that does change things, doesn't it?"

"I think so," Vicky agreed.

"Who's the witness?" Mitchell asked.

"It's Wilbur," Vicky admitted and Mitchell cringed immediately.

"The one with the glasses?" he asked hesitantly, he knew of Wilbur's faulty vision.

"Yes," Vicky nodded and glanced in the direction of the restaurant. "He's having coffee with Aunt Ida."

"I'll go talk with him," Mitchell said as he began to walk away from the desk, but paused a step or two away. When he glanced back Vicky realized she had been staring at him, because he looked right into her eyes. "Can we talk later?" he asked as he held her gaze.

"I think I just need to get all of this settled," Vicky uttered and glanced away. When she stole a glance back at him she could see his jaw clenched and his lips twitching over the battle of whether to say more or remain silent. Luckily, Sarah stepped into the lobby at that moment. Vicky excused herself and hurried over to Sarah. Sarah looked from Vicky to Mitchell and back to Vicky again.

"Wow, intense," she muttered as Mitchell walked towards the restaurant. "I guess you haven't ironed things out quite yet."

"I don't want to talk about it," Vicky said shortly as she turned to look at her sister. "There are more important things to deal with right now."

"Okay, okay," Sarah said quickly and held up her hands in a sign of surrender. "So what have you found out?"

"It looks like the main suspect is Mike. He's the only one that doesn't really have an alibi, and I'm pretty sure he's having an affair with Jane."

"Really?" Sarah asked as she studied Mike from across the room. He was standing close to his wife Charlene who had an arm wrapped around his waist in an offer of support. "Looks like she doesn't have a clue about it."

"Isn't it sad?" Vicky asked with a frown. "You can think you know someone, you can trust them, and they could be doing that behind your back."

"Not really," Sarah said softly. "I know my husband, and I know he would never do that to me."

Vicky glanced over at Sarah whose eyes were filled with certainty. Vicky wished she could understand what made that possible. Maybe it was just her suspicious, investigative nature, but she had a hard time believing that even the people she cared about the most weren't keeping secrets.

"We have this under control," Vicky assured Sarah and gave her sister a quick hug. "Go home, be with your family. If anything new comes up I'll let you know right away."

"Okay," Sarah nodded reluctantly. Vicky could tell that she was torn between staying or going. After Sarah left, Vicky walked into the restaurant to see if Mitchell was still talking to Wilbur, but she only found Aunt Ida and Wilbur at the table.

"Where's Mitchell?" Vicky asked curiously.

"He said he had all he needed," Aunt Ida shrugged. Vicky was a little hurt that he wouldn't have at least said goodbye to her.

"I told him everything I knew, but I wish I could be more helpful," Wilbur admitted with a sigh.

"You've already been a big help," Vicky assured him. "You went to a lot of effort."

"Anything for..." he hesitated a moment as he glanced at Aunt Ida before looking back at Vicky. "For the inn. It's like a second home to me, you know."

Vicky smiled warmly at his words. "I'm going to take a look outside around the pool again," she murmured.

"Be careful, Vicky," Aunt Ida cautioned as she met her niece's eyes. "If the murderer is still here at the inn then we could all be at risk."

"I will be," Vicky promised her as she headed for the door in the lobby that led out to the pool. The truth was she wanted a few minutes alone to try to sort things out.

Chapter Six

The pool and its surrounds had been processed by the crime scene technicians and Vicky pushed the crime scene tape to the side so she could walk through. As Vicky stepped out onto the pool deck she noticed the quiet. No one was outside having a glass of wine or contemplating an afternoon swim. The entire area held a sense of tragedy that was now made even more eerie by the knowledge that Simon had been murdered. Vicky stood beside the pool and stared down into the still water. As obvious as it seemed that Mike was the murderer, something still didn't sit right with Vicky. The argument she had overheard between Mike and Jane had left her very unsettled.

Then there was Alina's icy behavior, despite Lawrence's evident despair. She knew that Mitchell was working hard on the case, but the murder had occurred at her inn. She had been in the building when Simon was dying in the pool. She had to think about all of the little details she might have overlooked. She recalled the family gathered together beside the pool. They were laughing and having a great time one moment, and then arguing the next. They had turned from warm and friendly to bitter and volatile in the span of a few drinks.

Vicky tried to think back to what words were actually exchanged in the argument. She could recall that accusations flew about Jane, and that Simon had become furious. It sure seemed at the time that Simon loved his fiancée. But why would anyone kill Simon over a silly argument about his fiancée? Even if Mike was having an affair with her, was that enough to make him want to kill Simon? And what about Mike's wife, Charlene? She seemed like a mild and friendly woman, but perhaps she possessed enough strength to push a drunk Simon into the pool.

Vicky sighed and shook her head as the possibilities seemed endless. The family had a lot of history between them, and truly any one of them could be a suspect. Since they all had similar builds, the figure on the video tape offered no more of a hint. If only the cameras had been of better quality. She made a mental note to look into purchasing better cameras for the pool area. She decided it was time to speak more specifically with some of the family, off the record. If she could get Mike or Jane to admit to the affair then maybe she would get a hint as to who was responsible for Simon's death. As Vicky began to walk away from the pool, she heard Aunt Ida chatting with Wilbur just inside the lobby.

"You don't remember anything about what he looked like?" she was asking.

"I don't," he shook his head. "All I remember is his ball cap."

"Which all of the Carter men were wearing," Vicky pointed out as she stepped into the lobby. She paused beside the two and smiled kindly at Will. "I really appreciate how hard you're trying to figure all of this out," she said.

"I wish I could remember more," Will sighed with frustration. "I couldn't even really hear exactly what they were saying."

"Wait," Vicky paused a moment. "Maybe you can't remember the words, but do you remember anything about the voice? I know you said you can't tell the difference between the voices of the Carter men, but what about the tone or the volume?" she asked as she met Will's eyes through his thick glasses. Maybe vision wasn't his strong suit, but he might just have picked something up about the person's voice.

"Well," he frowned a little. "I remember that he sounded angry. He was growling his words, like he wanted to yell, but he was trying not to."

"And Simon?" Vicky pressed and listened closely as Will replied.

"Simon was sputtering, like he was shocked, or he just couldn't believe what the other man was saying. I wouldn't even say he was angry, he just seemed really surprised," he frowned and again shook his head. "I really do wish I could remember more."

"That's plenty," Vicky assured him as she smiled at him. "Just remember to stay with Aunt Ida, okay?" she said firmly. With Will being a potential witness and trying so hard to remember who the killer might be, and all of the suspects still staying in the inn she was worried that someone might try to hurt him. She knew that Aunt Ida would try to protect him, considering that she was almost fearless and was skilled in martial arts, and very protective of Will.

"Sure," he nodded and smiled shyly at Ida. "I don't mind one bit," he added.

Aunt Ida blushed a little and winked lightly. "I don't mind either."

As Vicky walked away from the lobby she thought about what Wilbur had said. If Simon had been surprised by whatever the person was saying then maybe it had been about an affair with Jane. Maybe she could shed more light on who the murderer was, maybe it was even Jane, herself. She decided that it was time for her to have a serious conversation with the woman who seemed to have caused such a deep rift in a family.

***

As Vicky stepped into the elevator she found Alina already waiting inside. "Going up?" Vicky asked as she pushed the button for the third floor.

"Yes," Alina sighed. "I was just trying to get a few minutes away from Lawrence. He's really a basket case over this."

Vicky eyed the woman with a hint of annoyance. "Well, he did just lose his son," she said as diplomatically as she could.

"Oh, I know he did," Alina waved her hand dismissively. "And honestly if that was what he was upset about then I would understand. But that's not even why he's upset."

"It's not?" Vicky asked with surprise. What could be worse than the murder of his son?

"He's so concerned about all the bad press," Alina sighed again and closed her eyes. "He's so worried about his image. That's the only reason he married me you know. He just wanted someone young on his arm who was intelligent enough not to embarrass him."

"I'm sorry," Vicky replied cautiously.

"Don't be," Alina smiled as she opened her eyes again. "I prefer a relationship that is more like a business deal. It gives us both the freedom to do as we please."

"You don't mean?" Vicky's voice trailed off as she knew it was none of her business.

"Affairs?" Alina smiled as she met Vicky's eyes. "Honey, men like Lawrence Carter can have any woman they want, any. I knew that when I married him, and I never expected that to change."

"And you're okay with that?" Vicky was a little shocked as the elevator came to a halt on the third floor.

"Remember the driver?" Alina asked with a light wink. "Lawrence has his forms of entertainment, and so do I. It's how our marriage works. Not everything is a fairytale, you know," she added as she stepped off the elevator. Vicky hesitated for a moment before following after her. It stunned her that Alina could be married to a man she obviously wasn't in love with, and not have a problem with his wandering desires. Was Simon that way, too? Maybe he wouldn't have even cared that his brother was sleeping with his future wife.

"So, I guess Mike has a wandering eye, too," Vicky suggested pensively as she caught up with Alina.

"Mike?" Alina burst out into a loud laugh. "No way. Charlene got a hold of him when he was in high school and she hasn't let him out of her sight since. He's nothing like his father," she paused a moment, a touch of affection entering her expression. "I might not be in my marriage for love, but I do admire Lawrence's children. Each one made their own way, especially Simon. He knew that he was his father's favorite, but he never leaned on Lawrence for favors or special treatment," she pursed her lips for a moment as if she was trying to hold back emotion, then slowly shook her head. "I just wish he would have had the chance to show Lawrence what it's like to be a good man. This is all just too tragic."

They paused outside the door to Alina's room and Vicky nodded sympathetically. "It certainly is unexpected when someone so young dies in such a terrible way," she pointed out.

"I wish it had been more unexpected," Alina admitted. "But I could swear that Lawrence knew something like this would happen. He was getting so nervous as we were getting ready to come here. He kept wondering if Simon would show up. I don't know why he was so concerned. He almost canceled the reunion at the last minute. I talked him out of it because, well," she sighed, her shoulders drooping slightly, "I just wanted a nice vacation and I had heard so many good things about this place."

Vicky nodded a little though she couldn't help but think that Lawrence might have had some kind of paternal instinct that the weekend would lead to disaster.

"Well, if you need anything feel free to call down to the front desk," Vicky insisted as Alina stepped into her room.

"Thank you," she smiled and disappeared into the room.

As Vicky walked down the hall towards Jane's room she caught sight of Charlene at the ice machine.

"Hi Charlene, how are you doing?" Vicky asked as she paused beside her and offered to carry the ice for her.

"I've got it," Charlene said sternly and hugged the bucket of ice. "Mike just wants a few cocktails in the room," she admitted.

"How are you two holding up?" Vicky pressed with growing concern.

"As best as can be expected," Charlene replied with a slight shake of her head. "Mike cared so deeply for his brother," she frowned. Vicky was surprised by that comment.

"Oh, were they close?" she asked with disbelief.

"Of course they were," Charlene narrowed her eyes a little. "Why wouldn't you think they were?"

"Well, it's just I heard them arguing..." Vicky began to explain, her voice wavering slightly as she tried to disguise her deeper suspicions about Mike's behavior with Jane.

"Oh that," Charlene rolled her eyes and then shifted the ice bucket from one arm to the other. "The truth is Mike played a big part in raising

Simon. See, Lawrence was always too busy. Even though Mike was only a few years older he took responsibility for Simon. We got together in high school, not long after Lawrence divorced his first wife. Mike was a little broken up about it, he was really hurt that his father had been cheating on his mother," she drew her lips into a thin line of disgust. "Some people have no idea what a real loving relationship is supposed to be like."

Vicky swallowed back the words that were rising to her lips. She felt almost compelled to reveal what Mike had been up to behind closed doors with Jane. But the way that Charlene described Mike was very different from Vicky's impression of him. She nodded encouragingly as she could tell that Charlene had more to say.

"After that, Mike started to become really protective of Simon. If Simon wanted to date someone we had to double with them. Of course, when Simon reached college all that changed. Jane is the first girlfriend that Simon found all on his own. Mike had it in his head and still does that Jane was just after Simon for his money, that she was just manipulating him, and that she would take him for all he was worth and then leave him," Charlene rolled her eyes and shook her head. "I tried to tell him that the more Mike tried to pull them apart, the more Simon would want to be with her, but he is so stubborn. He just kept saying that he had to protect his brother, and if no one else would tell him the truth, then he would."

"Did he?" Vicky asked as she moved slightly closer to Charlene. "Did he tell Simon his suspicions?"

"He hinted at it. He kept trying to catch Jane in the act. It got so bad that he even hired a private detective."

"Wow," Vicky said and then raised her eyebrows. "He was really serious about getting some proof."

"That's the strange thing," Charlene admitted thoughtfully. "He hired the private detective, and then one day I asked him if the detective had found anything because his mood had changed, he'd become really quiet. He said no, and not to bring it up again," she glanced towards the door of the room they were staying in. "Before all of this I could have told you every single thought in Mike's head, but since then, he's been closed off to me," she blinked as if she suddenly realized just how much she was sharing with Vicky. "Oh I'm sorry, listen to me ramble. My point is, Mike adored Simon, and yes they argued over Jane, but that was only because Mike was trying to protect his little brother."

"No wonder he's taking it so hard," Vicky shook her head. "Please make sure to let me know if there's anything at all I can do to make this time a little easier."

"I will," Charlene nodded. "I think he just wishes the crime would get solved and that we could all move on."

"I can understand that," Vicky nodded. But she wondered if that could really be what Mike wanted. If he was the one who killed his brother he probably wished the crime would remain unsolved. Just as Vicky was about to ask Charlene about Mike's change in behavior, Mike opened the door to the room.

"Char, do you have the ice?" he asked and passed his bloodshot eyes over Vicky. He curled his lip in a drunken attempt at a smile. "Did my wife give her permission to be questioned?" he asked, stumbling over his words.

"Mike, don't," Charlene warned him. "Look I have a whole bucket of ice," she said as she walked towards him.

"Don't be nice to her, Charlene. She thinks I killed my own brother, " he chuckled, the laughter sliced up by bitterness.

"Of course, she doesn't think that Mike," Charlene huffed as she steered her inebriated husband back into the room. She mouthed 'sorry' over her shoulder to Vicky, who nodded slightly. As the door to their room closed, Vicky wondered if Mike had simply been too drunk to realize the gravity of what he was doing. Had it been a crime of passion? Had Mike wanted to protect his brother so badly that he killed him in order to keep him away from Jane?

It made no sense to Vicky, but then she had never been as drunk as Mike obviously was. As she walked down the hallway towards Jane's room, she wondered how she would initiate the conversation with her. She didn't want to isolate her as she might be her only ally. When she knocked lightly on the door it opened immediately. Jane stared at her, her beautiful visage pale and shadowed by grief. She stepped back to allow her inside without Vicky even having to explain why she was there. Vicky stepped inside and Jane closed the door behind her.

"I heard what she was saying out there," Jane said glumly as she crossed her arms across her stomach. "I'm just the resident manipulative whore," she rolled her eyes which glistened with tears.

"People just say things," Vicky offered in a sympathetic tone. "All Charlene said was that Mike was really protective of Simon."

"He was," Jane admitted and a tear slid down her cheek. "He really was," she whispered.

Vicky studied her for a long moment. She knew that it was the perfect time to ask the question she had in mind, but she still felt a little uneasy about it.

"So, you and Mike, you weren't having an affair?" Vicky blurted out, though she tried to even out her words. Jane took a slight step back and raised her eyes to Vicky. The mixture of emotions that crossed her features made it clear that she was stunned by the question.

"What are you talking about?" Jane asked sharply as she glared at Vicky. "How could you even say such a thing?"

"Am I wrong?" Vicky asked. She knew that she had already crossed a line. There was no turning back now. "Because I overheard you and Mike, Jane, I heard you arguing."

"You know," Jane shook her head and raised a hand to her mouth to cover a gasp. "I expect this from the Carters, they don't get it. But you?" she glowered at Vicky. "You're not one of these, born with a silver spoon in your mouth, types. Yet, you still think the same thing about me? That I must have been cheating on Simon?"

"The argument," Vicky pressed, not letting the woman's emotional words sway her. "I heard it. There's no getting around that."

"There is if you had no clue what we were talking about. That's what being nosy will get you, an earful of nonsense," she shook her head and opened the door to her room. "I trust you can find your own way out."

"Jane, I'm just trying to get to the bottom of things," Vicky insisted as she stared into the woman's eyes.

"Well, I'll make it easy for you, Vicky," Jane replied as she continued to hold the door open. "I was not sleeping with Mike, and I did not kill my fiancé. Now, could you please leave?"

Vicky held her gaze for a moment longer before turning and stepping out of the room. Jane pushed the door closed behind her. Vicky found herself standing in the empty hallway a little stunned by everything she had learned. Not only did Charlene deny the affair, but Jane did, too. Was it just a front to throw her off? But if Jane had been involved in the murder it would have benefited her to throw Mike under the bus. There was only one person she hadn't talked to yet that might be able to shed a little more light on the situation. She turned around to walk back down the hallway and discovered that Lawrence had just stepped out of the elevator. He locked eyes with Vicky from a few feet away and stopped in his tracks.

"Mr. Carter," Vicky said and cleared her throat as she walked towards him.

"Everything's fine, I don't need anything," he said dismissively as he began to walk past her to get to his room.

"If you don't mind I was wondering if I could ask you a few questions," Vicky suggested calmly.

"You're not a police officer, are you?" he asked with a furrowed brow.

"No sir, I'm not," Vicky replied in a more professional tone. "However, I do like to keep track of what happens at the inn, and if we were in any way negligent…"

"Is that what this is about?" he snapped as he glared at her. "Are you afraid that I'm going to sue you or something?"

Vicky was silent as she nodded.

"Look, do you have some paper I can sign?" he asked with a mild shrug. "Unless you're the one that pushed him in the pool I don't see how the inn could be responsible."

"Sure, I have a waiver," Vicky offered even though she did not have anything of the kind.

"Well, then come on in and I'll sign it for you. Anything to stop being asked questions," he sighed and pulled his cap off briefly to run his hand back over his balding scalp.

"Okay, thank you," Vicky said quickly and he opened the door to his room for her. Alina was sitting on the couch flipping through her phone when they stepped inside. She barely glanced up at the two as Lawrence walked over to the kitchen counter. Vicky was a little flustered as she realized that now she had to produce the form she claimed to have. She searched through her purse for it and then frowned.

"I'm sorry, I thought I had it with me," she shook her head and looked up at Lawrence who sighed heavily.

"Just go and get it, make it quick," he insisted. "I have an important call to make at three."

Vicky glanced up at the alarm clock to see what time it was. She was startled by what she saw on the clock. She glanced at her watch and then back at the clock.

"Oh, it looks like your clock is off," Vicky said with a frown as she walked over to it.

"Oh, uh, yeah looks like it is," he said with a mild shrug. "I don't pay attention to those things. I prefer to use my watch," he explained.

"Oh, I see," Vicky said as she adjusted the time so that it was correct. Then she noticed something on the floor. It was a tiny piece of gold. She stared at it for a long moment. Then she turned and pretended that her purse had slid off her shoulder. As it fell to the floor a few of its contents scattered across the floor. She reached down and picked them up quickly.

"So sorry," she mumbled as she cleaned up.

"It's fine, like I said, I just can't miss this call," he said impatiently. Vicky made sure she picked up the tiny bit of gold as well.

"Don't worry about the form," she said quickly. "We can take care of that when you check out. I'll make sure everyone knows that you're not to be disturbed, okay?"

"Perfect," he smiled with relief and then walked her to the door. As Vicky stepped out into the hall again she didn't bother to look over her shoulder at Lawrence, in fact she did her best not to look at him at all. Instead she headed straight for the elevator.

Chapter Seven

Vicky rode the elevator down to the lobby, her mind spinning with what she suspected. As she walked over to the front desk she found Aunt Ida and Wilbur waiting for her.

"How are you doing, sweetie?" Aunt Ida asked as she noticed the concern reflected in Vicky's features.

"Honestly," Vicky shook her head as she set her purse down on the counter. "Not so great."

"What's wrong?" Wilbur asked as he leaned closer to her.

"I just have this crazy suspicion," Vicky shook her head slightly. "But it just couldn't be true."

"Hmm," Aunt Ida met Vicky's eyes intently. "Never doubt your instincts, Vicky, you get them from me after all," she winked lightly at Vicky.

"Maybe you're right, Aunt Ida," Vicky smiled a little as she began fishing through her purse for the bit of broken gold she had found. When she pulled it out of her purse Wilbur took off his glasses.

"What's that you've got there?" he asked curiously.

"I'm not sure," Vicky admitted. "Do either of you know what it is?"

Wilbur leaned very close to the gold and narrowed his eyes so that he could see it clearly. "Oh sure, it looks like a piece of a watch winding stem."

"What's a winding stem?" Vicky asked with some confusion.

"It's the part of the watch that lets you set the time. You need it to wind it manually on mechanical watches. If you pull it out to wind the watch or set the time and leave it out, your watch stops," he explained. "Most people have those newfangled digital watches. I'd venture to say this came from a more expensive watch, from someone who appreciates a classic."

"Like Jane's watch," Vicky murmured under her breath as she recalled how Jane had said her watch stopped and it looked as if it was damaged.

"Are you on to something?" Aunt Ida asked curiously as she studied Vicky.

"I'm not sure yet," Vicky admitted as she pulled out her cell phone. "The two of you just stick together, okay?"

"Absolutely," Aunt Ida nodded as she looped her arm through Wilbur's. "We're going to have tea and cookies in the garden."

"Tea and cookies?" Vicky asked with mirth in her eyes.

"What?" Aunt Ida asked with a huff. "I can be fancy."

"If you say so," Vicky found herself grinning as the two walked away. As she stood beside the front desk she texted Mitchell explaining what she had found. She was beginning to suspect that Jane and Lawrence's alibi might have been less solid than they first assumed. After sending the text she tucked the piece of watch into her pocket and left her purse and cell phone behind the desk. She wanted to take another look at the pool area now that the crime scene tape had been removed.

As Vicky stepped out onto the pool deck she could hear Aunt Ida and Wilbur talking softly as they walked to the small patio area set up in the center of the garden to enjoy their afternoon snack.

Vicky noticed right away that a bench was still out of place. She walked over to it and tested the weight of it. It was a metal bench, not a plastic one, so it was rather hard to slide. She guessed that it had been pushed in the middle of a struggle or maybe even by the crime scene techs. Vicky crouched down low and saw where the bench had been slid back across the pool deck. She was certain she had straightened everything up before the Carters had lunch out on the pool deck, so it must have been moved after that. As she slid it back into place she caught a glimmer in between the wooden decking out of the corner of her eye.

She crouched down again and carefully removed the item that was wedged between the boards. It was a golden chain along with a pendant. She recognized the pendant immediately because it was circular with a raised golden C. It was the pendant that Lawrence Carter had been wearing the day he checked into the inn. If the bench had been disturbed during a confrontation with Simon, then surely the pendant had been pulled off during that same confrontation. Which meant that Lawrence was most likely the other person who had been on the camera. The police must have missed the pendant because it was lodged quite far down and only visible from a particular angle.

A chill ran down Vicky's spine as she remembered Lawrence's comment about Simon being pushed into the pool. No one had stated that Simon was pushed, but that was a reasonable assumption to make. What wasn't reasonable was Lawrence's necklace being lost and he never mentioning that it was missing. The evidence was beginning to pile up, and it was all pointing in the direction of Lawrence. That realization sunk in slowly as Vicky stared at the pendant. Could she really accuse a father of killing his own child? There had to be some other explanation, she tried to tell herself. But she knew that there wasn't.

Vicky stood up and held tightly to the pendant. She would talk to Mitchell about it first. Maybe he could offer her some kind of alternative theory. She reached into her pocket for her phone, and then recalled leaving it behind the front desk. As she walked back towards the lobby of the inn she heard footsteps walking up behind her. Vicky smiled and tucked the necklace into her pocket as she turned, expecting it to be Wilbur or Aunt Ida.

"Vicky!" Lawrence called out as he came to a halt right behind her. "I'm glad I caught you."

Vicky's heart began to race, her eyes widened slightly. She tried to arrange her features in a friendly expression, but it was hard not to immediately judge the man she now believed had killed his son.

"How can I help you, Mr. Carter?" she asked with a smile.

"I was looking for Alina," Lawrence explained as he studied her intently. "We had a bit of a spat and she took off. I haven't seen her since."

"Maybe she's getting a massage," Vicky replied calmly, trying to keep her nerves from showing. "She did enquire about the masseuse we have available on Sundays."

"Oh, I see," Lawrence smiled along with a chuckle that made Vicky twitch. "That would be where she is then. She never passes up a massage."

"Right," Vicky nodded curtly, eager to get away from him, at least until she could plan out a way to confront him. "I can arrange one for you as well if you would like."

"No, that's fine," Lawrence glanced at the hand she had covering her right pocket. A small amount of the chain of the necklace had slid through two of her fingers.

"What do you have there?" he asked curiously. Instinctively he reached up to his neck. When he discovered that there was no chain or pendant there his expression tensed. "What is that?" he asked again in a more strained voice.

"It's a necklace," she replied hesitantly. She pulled it from her pocket and intended to pretend that she didn't know it was his. "I just found it, and was going to take it to lost and found," she explained as the pendant with the golden C broke free of her pocket. She heard a slight clatter as the broken watch winding stem fell out with it.

"That's mine," he said quietly and then crouched down to pick up the stem. As soon as he realized what was in his hand he grimaced. He scowled as he studied her.

"And what's this?" he asked.

She hadn't planned to confront him just yet but he was forcing her to. "Oh, I just found it on the floor," Vicky began to explain casually. Her heart was really pounding and she regretted leaving her cell phone behind the desk.

"In my room?" he asked, his tone taking on an eerie calm.

"I think so," Vicky replied as she opened her hand and let the necklace drop into his open palm. "Here, have your necklace back."

"Where did you find it?" Lawrence asked gruffly, his eyes boring into hers as he stood to his full height.

"By the pool," she replied, her voice barely above a whisper. She did her best to avoid looking directly at him.

"By the pool," he repeated in that eerie tone, and took a step closer to her. "I suppose that makes you think some crazy things."

"No, of course not," Vicky said quickly. "I'm sure you just lost it during lunch. Or maybe after," she added and started to move past him towards the lobby. Lawrence caught her by the arm, his grip much firmer than she expected it to be.

"Tell me what you suspect, Vicky," Lawrence commanded and she was abruptly aware of the power he must wield in the corporation he ran. He expected her to comply without resistance.

"I'm just going to let the police sort all of this out," she said casually and started to pull away. When she felt his firm hand curling around her shoulder her heart sunk. She knew that this was not a confrontation that she was going to be able to avoid. He was not going to believe that she didn't suspect him.

"You're not going to tell the police about the necklace or the watch piece, Vicky," he hissed and tried to spin her around to face him. Vicky lunged hard and managed to tear away from him. When she felt her freedom she took off at a sprint down the narrow path that led to the garden. She knew that Aunt Ida had said she was going to spend an hour or so with Will in the garden and she would have her phone with her. If she could get to her, she could call for help, and hopefully Lawrence would think twice about hurting her with two witnesses present.

"Get back here!" Lawrence growled while trying not to shout from anger. He chased after her. Despite his age he was very fit, and Vicky could hear him closing in on her.

"Do you think you're going to get away from me?" Lawrence barked after her as she reached the edge of the garden. She couldn't run any farther without jumping over tall bushes that surrounded the garden.

"There are people in the garden!" she said very loudly hoping Aunt Ida would hear her. "I know you don't want to hurt me, Lawrence," she said again, louder than she needed to.

"Are you talking about dear Aunt Ida and old Wilbur?" Lawrence chuckled as he stepped closer to her, his eyes gleaming with danger. "I sent them inside before I stopped to talk to you. I told them that you were looking for them, had some information about the case."

Vicky's heart sunk as she realized that he had planned the entire confrontation. He must have suspected something when she spotted the alarm clock being the wrong time. Now she truly was alone, and far enough from the inn that no one would hear her if she screamed.

"Lawrence, let's just go back to the inn and talk about this," she said as calmly as she could. She hoped he couldn't tell that she was trembling.

"We're not going back to the inn, Vicky," he said in that low growl that left her so unsettled. "As far as anyone knows, I'm with Jane, and that's how it will stay. No one will come looking for you," he added.

"You do know how to set up an alibi, don't you?" Vicky asked, her voice becoming less panicked and more determined. "Isn't that what you did with Jane before? Jane didn't even know about it, did she?"

Lawrence glowered at her, the intensity growing in his gaze. "You used her for your alibi. You broke the winding stem so she would think it was a certain time, you even changed the alarm clock, so that it would trick her, too," she narrowed her eyes and shook her head slowly. "You are a cunning man. I can see how you made your millions, but what I can't understand is why?"

Lawrence lowered his eyes at the question but Vicky pushed him harder. She was hoping that if she could keep him talking, eventually someone would come looking for her. Lawrence was tall and muscular. His age did not make him vulnerable in any way. Vicky wasn't sure if she would be able to overpower him. "How could you do it?" she asked as she stared at him. "Why would you do it? He was your son," she shook her head as she studied him. "Simon didn't deserve to die, did he?" her voice strangled with disgust.

"Don't judge me," Lawrence growled as he stepped closer to her. "You have no idea what it's like. When you have a fortune everyone wants a piece of it. You're not just a man, you're a treasure chest, and everyone around you will pick you clean if you're not careful."

"It was all over the pre-nuptial?" Vicky asked incredulously. "Did you find out about the affair she was having with Mike?"

"With Mike?" Lawrence sputtered out. "For being so nosy, you've got it all wrong," Lawrence chuckled and shook his head. "Mike hasn't touched another woman since he married that busy body Charlene. She keeps tabs on him, and he has this crazy notion in his head that he's in love with her. Jane was not having an affair with Mike," he shook his head again as if it was the stupidest thing he had ever heard.

Vicky was a little surprised by this. She was certain that Jane was having an affair with someone, otherwise what sense did the argument make that she had overheard? Was it possible that Lawrence simply didn't know about the affair? A moment later it dawned on her and her eyes widened further.

"It was you," she hissed as she narrowed her eyes, her stomach flipped with even more disgust. "You're the one that was having an affair with Jane."

"Guilty," Lawrence smirked as if he was somewhat proud of his actions. "I have to admit, it started out as a way to get my son to turn against her, but I can see what he saw in her now. She's a very seductive woman."

Vicky grimaced with disgust at his words. "But she was your son's fiancée," she reminded him. "Aren't there enough other women in the world that you could have just left her alone?"

"Yes, she was my son's fiancée. From the wrong class, the wrong type of woman. All the more reason to prove how disloyal she is," Lawrence sighed and shifted his weight from one foot to the other, he was watching her closely to make sure she didn't try to push past him. "She was more than happy to have an affair with me, so why would I let my son marry a woman like that?" he frowned and his jaw clenched for a moment as if he was recalling a painful memory. "But he was just so stubborn. I thought telling him the truth would finally knock some sense into him. He was so insistent that she not have to sign a pre-nuptial. They weren't even married yet and she was already cheating on him with his own father! But when I told him..."

"He had a different reaction, didn't he?" Vicky asked as her heartbeat quickened. "He knew that you conned her into it."

"He got so angry," Lawrence admitted with a sigh. "I tried to explain to him how I was trying to help him, to protect him. For once I was trying to be a father and protect my child from certain heartbreak and financial ruin. You would think he would thank me for that, but instead he was furious. He put his hands on me, accusing me of manipulating Jane and taking everything from him. The way he was shouting and carrying on, I knew someone was bound to hear. I couldn't have the rest of the family know that I was sleeping with Jane. He was out of control!"

"So, you tried to control him," Vicky suggested, her throat tightening with horror at the thought of it. "You tried to quiet him down."

Lawrence lowered his eyes and his cheeks flushed with shame. "I never expected him to slip. I never expected it, I just wanted him to be quiet. I told him to shut his disrespectful mouth and he spat at me! He said I was the reason the family was split apart, and now I was trying to do the same thing to him and Jane," he shook his head and closed his eyes. "When he wouldn't quiet down I just gave him a shove but he fought back," he murmured his words. "I just wanted to get my point across and he was refusing to listen to any kind of reason, I didn't expect..." his words trailed off for a moment before he reluctantly began to speak again. "His head cracked against the tiles by the pool," he breathed his words out. "He just fell, and then he was just gone," he swallowed thickly. "He wasn't even bleeding, but he had no life in him. No pulse, he wasn't breathing, I knew he was dead," his final word wavered slightly but not enough for Vicky to believe that he was genuinely heartbroken over the loss of his son.

"So, you decided to cover up what you did," Vicky challenged him taking a daring step forward so that there was only a small amount of space between the two of them.

"I did," Lawrence murmured. "I couldn't have word getting out that I had killed my own son, even if it was his own fault really," he shook his head and muttered something under his breath before continuing. "So, I rolled him into the pool," he glanced in the direction of the pool. "I didn't think anyone would investigate the death too deeply. I figured it would all be swept under the rug," he gritted his teeth as he looked back at Vicky. "Which is exactly what should have happened. Then we wouldn't be in the messy situation we are in right now."

"I can't believe you just pushed him in and walked away," Vicky hissed with a scowl of repulsion. "Your own son, just like that!"

"Yes," he replied and then cleared his throat. "I would prefer it if he wasn't dead, but that's just not how things worked out," he shrugged as if it was a business deal that had gone south. "I would have preferred that you not go snooping around and put yourself in this dangerous position, but you did," he moved closer to her, his thick shoulders and broad chest making a wall in front of her. "So, now you're going to have to suffer the consequences for your nosy behavior."

"You're digging a hole for yourself, Lawrence," Vicky said coolly. "One that you're not going to climb out of."

"Funny thing about holes," Lawrence growled as he pulled a gun from the back of his pants. "If you dig them deep enough, no one ever finds them."

"Lawrence, you don't have to do this," Vicky said quickly as the afternoon sunlight flashed off the smooth barrel of the gun. "Just put the gun away. What happened to Simon was an accident, like you said, at the very worst it will be considered a crime of passion. But if you kill me, there's no turning back from that. No one is going to believe..."

"They won't need to," he reminded her as he raised the gun in the air. "Because they won't find you," he pointed the gun directly at her and then steered her away from the bushes towards the garden shed. With each step that Vicky took she knew it might be her last. She contemplated screaming, but there was no way anyone could get to her before he pulled the trigger. They were too far from the inn for anyone to hear her anyway. He jerked her towards the shed and then swung open the door, which of course the gardener had left open. As he pushed her inside he grabbed the padlock and hooked it over the latch on the door, essentially locking them inside. That was when Vicky realized Lawrence had no intentions of letting her leave the shed alive.

"Lawrence," Vicky attempted to get his attention again, to steer him away from the determination he seemed to have to kill her. "Just think this through," she pleaded with him. "You're a reasonable man. You know that you can afford to hire the best lawyers in the country. You will likely get acquitted."

"That may all be true, Vicky," he said calmly as he studied her with a hint of resentment for the trouble that she was putting him through. "But what you don't understand is that even the rumor of me being involved in my son's death would ruin me. It would ruin the reputation of my entire family," he added and then sighed as he leaned against the wall of the shed. "And really, how is that fair?" he asked as he tilted his head to the side and studied her. "I mean, do we all have to suffer because of Simon's screw up?"

"It wasn't Simon's fault," Vicky growled with frustration. "If you're going to kill me, fine, but there is no excuse you can use to justify killing me. Just as there is no excuse you can use to justify killing your own son."

"Simon was a good kid," Lawrence admitted with a mild shrug. "He had a lot of potential, and a lot of spirit. But he had terrible taste in women. If he had simply listened to me, then he might have saved his own life. I warned him against Jane. When he refused to comply with breaking up with her, I started an affair with her, with the purpose of showing Simon just how foolish he was being."

"I bet you were very proud of yourself," Vicky said quietly. "Did you know that Mike knew about your little fling with your future daughter-in-law?"

"Mike knows?" Lawrence asked with surprise. "Well, that's one juicy tidbit that I didn't know about. Maybe your nosiness came in handy after all. I bet Mike wasn't too happy about it," he chuckled. "No, I'm sure he wasn't. Mike always babied Simon."

"You mean raised him?" Vicky pointed out. "That's why he and Mike were arguing, because Mike knew about the affair and couldn't bring himself to tell the truth about who Jane was having an affair with. You know, I think the strangest part of this entire story is that your sons loved you, in spite of who you are."

"And Mike still does," Lawrence pointed out. "And he always will as long as you never have the chance to tell the truth."

Vicky braced herself for what she knew would come next. She was certain that there was only one thing loud and strange enough to alert someone to her predicament. But getting her hands on it was going to be very difficult. Luckily she spotted something that Lawrence wasn't paying any attention to. It was a large metal rake, and it was leaning across a stack of old pots. The end of the handle was just close enough to Vicky that she could step on the end of it. She waited until Lawrence raised the gun again. Then she stepped hard on the handle, sending the metal rake up into the air. It smacked Lawrence hard in the elbow of the arm that was holding the gun.

"Ouch," he yelped and jerked his arm upward as Vicky had hoped he would. As his hand jerked upward the gun went off, very loudly. Lawrence got control of the gun and glared at Vicky.

"Wrong move," he growled at her and then pointed to a piece of landscaping wood. "Sit down," he commanded her. "Your little stunt won't get you anywhere. No one is going to think much about one gunshot. They'll think it was a car backfiring, or someone playing with fireworks. No one is going to come looking for you," he insisted as Vicky reluctantly sat down. "So, now you and I, we're going to wait here until it gets dark. Then I can shoot you and bury you, and be ready for my flight home tomorrow."

"I wouldn't count on it," Vicky countered, her eyes narrowed as she met his gaze boldly. She wasn't going to allow him to frighten her, even though she couldn't stop her heart from racing.

Chapter Eight

The shot that rang out over the manicured grounds of the inn was not one that could be easily dismissed. Not when someone who lived in the inn had started her very own murder-mystery book club. As soon as Ida heard it, she gasped. She looked over at Wilbur whose eyes had widened. They had been inside the inn for about five minutes looking for Vicky after Lawrence had indicated that she needed to speak with them. But there was no sign of her, other than her purse and phone being behind the front desk.

When Ida heard the shot ring out her stomach churned. She hoped that it had nothing to do with Vicky, but deep down she knew it did. As she started to walk towards the sound, her cell phone began to ring. She still had a hard time managing the thing, but now at least she could tell that it was Mitchell calling.

"Ida, I'm so sorry if I disturbed you, I've been calling Vicky for the past fifteen minutes and she hasn't answered. I just wanted to make sure she was safe."

"Oh dear, Mitchell, I don't think she is," Ida replied in a shaky voice. "I believe I just heard a gunshot."

"A gunshot?" Mitchell asked with surprise. "Ida, stay where you are, I'll be there in a few minutes." Aunt Ida agreed but she had no intention of staying put. She knew that Vicky needed her help.

"Wilbur, will you do me a favor?" she asked as she turned to look at the man who was quickly becoming a close friend.

"Anything for you, Ida," he replied with a soft smile.

"Will you please wait here for Mitchell? I don't want him to be worried if he arrives and can't find us," she explained.

"Sure," he nodded and then hesitated. "But Ida, make sure you don't get yourself into any kind of trouble."

"Oh honey," Ida smiled as she kissed his cheek swiftly. "It's trouble that needs to look out for me."

As she walked out of the lobby towards the garden, she wondered where exactly the gunshot had come from. She had initially heard it inside the inn so it was hard to place. What wasn't hard to place was the garden shed being closed and locked. The new gardener was a bit of a slob, and not very good at remembering to lock up the shed. It certainly struck Ida as odd that it would be locked. As she stepped closer to it she could hear voices inside. She was relieved to hear Vicky's voice but she could tell by the tone of it that she was in trouble. Ida looked for the key to the padlock, but it was nowhere to be found.

"You'll never get away with this," she heard Vicky growl from inside the shed.

"That's where you're wrong," Lawrence chuckled in response, and then growled his words. "I already have." Aunt Ida was shocked to discover it was Lawrence Carter holding Vicky in the shed, but she didn't allow that revelation to distract her. She had to find a way to get Vicky out of that shed.

Ida crept up to the side of the shed. There was a window that was closed on that side of the shed. She rose up on her toes and peered through it. She could see Vicky towards the back of the shed, and Lawrence towering over her. Then she noticed the gun in his hand. So, that was where the gunshot had come from. Aunt Ida shuddered at the idea of Vicky being held at gunpoint.

Ida looked around for something she might be able to use as a weapon. She spotted a trowel laying on the ground beside the shed and for once was grateful for the gardener's disregard for cleaning up his tools. She picked up the trowel and then walked up to the window. It was just slightly higher than her line of sight. She reluctantly tipped over a clay flower pot that was filled with daffodils into a bucket that was filled with water. "Sorry for the drowning," she said to the daffodils and then she climbed on top of the clay pot.

Aunt Ida was high enough then to open the window slightly. She opened it just far enough that it wouldn't be noticed by those inside the shed. She didn't want to alert Lawrence to her presence and have him do something to hurt Vicky before she could protect her. She aimed the trowel carefully at the back of the man's head. Then, using all of her might she flung it towards the back of his head. Lawrence gasped in pain when the metal trowel struck his head. He reached up and knocked the cap off he was wearing. He grasped the back of his head and groaned in pain.

Vicky moved quickly and snatched up a nearby shovel. She swung it hard against Lawrence's head. Lawrence cried out in pain again and stumbled backwards. He tripped over a pile of bags filled with fertilizer and fell backwards landing hard on his back. In the same moment Aunt Ida climbed through the window and into the shed. She jumped down into the shed just in time to see Lawrence fall.

"Good shot, Vicky," she said with genuine admiration.

"Thanks," Vicky winced as she kicked the gun from Lawrence's hand. He was not quite out cold, but he was dazed. She carefully picked up the gun off the floor and then looked at Aunt Ida with relief.

"Let's get out of here," Ida said quickly and turned back to the window. But as she had climbed inside she had knocked it out of place with her foot. It had fallen closed. When she tried to open it again it was jammed.

"It's stuck," Aunt Ida growled. Vicky joined her in trying to pry the window up but it wouldn't budge.

"We can just break it," Vicky suggested and picked up the trowel that had fallen on the floor. She struck the glass hard with it, but it didn't even leave a scratch.

"It's no use," Aunt Ida sighed and then looked towards the door of the shed. "Let's see if we can get the door to bend open far enough."

Both she and Vicky pushed hard on the door. But it wouldn't budge even an inch. Aunt Ida stopped to think as Vicky continued to shove against the door.

"Oh no," Vicky frowned as she pushed hard against the door of the shed. "There's no way out of here!"

"Vicky?" a familiar voice called out from outside the shed. "Are you in there?"

"I'm in here," Vicky called back as she pounded on the door. "It's locked. We can't get out. Lawrence is in here with us, he's the one that killed Simon!"

"Don't worry, I'm here," Mitchell said quickly and tugged at the door of the shed.

"That's it, I've had enough," Lawrence gasped as he regained his senses. Only then did Vicky realize she had made the grave mistake of leaving the shovel beside the man. As she turned around she saw him swinging the shovel down towards Aunt Ida's head.

"No!" Vicky shouted and raised the gun to shoot at Lawrence but before she could he struck her hand with the shovel, knocking the gun out of her grasp.

Mitchell could hear the struggle from outside and was determined to get inside to protect Vicky and Ida. Mitchell leaned his weight against the door of the shed. He could feel it give enough that he knew he would be able to get inside with one well-aimed bullet. But he had to be cautious because Ida and Vicky were inside. Inside the shed Vicky and Lawrence were both scrambling for the gun that had skidded across the floor.

Lawrence got to the gun first and grasped it tightly.

"Vicky?" Mitchell called through the door. "Vicky can you hear me?" he shouted again.

"Yes," she growled as she tried to bend Lawrence's hand backwards far enough to force him to release the gun while Aunt Ida climbed on his back trying to wrestle him to the ground. Her arms and legs wrapped around him.

"Stand back," Mitchell commanded from outside the shed. Aunt Ida managed to get Lawrence to the ground and then the three continued to wrestle for the gun. Aunt Ida reached out and grabbed a handful of fertilizer from an open bag. Then she flung it into Lawrence's face.

"Ugh," he sputtered and lost focus on the weapon for a moment. Vicky managed to get the gun from his hand but as she started to stand up, Lawrence grabbed the shovel again. Before she could say a word about it Mitchell had fired a bullet through the locking mechanism on the door.

"Mitchell, watch out!" Vicky cried out in an attempt to warn him about Lawrence and the shovel. Mitchell slammed his weight into the door and it sprung inward just in time to strike the shovel that Lawrence was raising, and knock it backwards into his own face.

"Ow," Lawrence groaned as he sunk down to his knees and held his nose which had been hit by the door. Mitchell immediately wrenched the shovel from his grasp and tossed it aside. He pinned Lawrence to the ground, handcuffed him, and read him his rights. As Vicky watched his sharp and well-practiced movements, she was reminded of just how good he was at his job. If he hadn't shown up at that exact moment, who knew what might have happened. Lawrence certainly had no intention of ever letting them out of the shed alive.

"Thank you, Mitchell," Aunt Ida said quickly, covering Vicky's silence as she stared at him. "I would have managed to take him out soon enough though."

Mitchell pulled Lawrence to his feet. He didn't spare the man a single glance as he guided him out of the shed, but his eyes did lock briefly on Vicky's. Vicky held his gaze in return, and he searched her green eyes until he was satisfied that she was okay, before he pushed Lawrence out of the shed. Vicky felt her heart flutter as he walked out the door. She had so much that she wanted to say, but wasn't quite sure how to say it. As Mitchell walked Lawrence down the path, around the pool, and back towards the inn, the older man began to speak.

"He was going to ruin everything," he muttered with absolute disdain. "He was going to give his fortune, my fortune, away to some girl," he growled in disgust.

"Some girl?" Jane snapped as she stood between Lawrence, Mitchell, and the inn. "Is that what you're going to say?" she asked with tears in her eyes. She must have overheard some of the commotion and had come outside to see what was happening. "You were the one who came to me, Lawrence. You seduced me, you told me that you loved me! You said that Simon was sleeping around, that he didn't know how to value a real good woman. You put so many horrible thoughts into my head," she sighed as she wiped at her eyes. "But it was my own fault for believing them."

"I just wanted to prove to my son what a whore you really were," Lawrence sneered and then raked his eyes across her from top to bottom. "The worst part is, even when I told him what you and I had been doing, he still came to your defense. Claimed that I must have forced you, or manipulated you. I never did understand that boy. I guess all of Mike's babying of him finally ruined him," he shook his head as Mitchell gave him a firm shove towards the sidewalk that led to the parking lot.

"Well, you'll have plenty of time to think about it," Mitchell promised as he walked him the rest of the way to the police car that was waiting. Vicky and Ida followed after him, with Jane trailing a few steps behind. As Mitchell pressed his hand to the top of Lawrence's head to help guide him into the back seat of the car, a crowd began to gather outside the inn. It was Mike, and his wife, along with his cousins and their husbands. Lawrence's brother and his wife were also there. Alina was the last to step outside. Alina turned to face Jane and narrowed her eyes as she studied her.

"Well, how do you feel now, Jane?" Alina asked. "You still want to act like you're better than me?" Jane glanced away as a blush rose in her cheeks. It was clear that she was troubled by how things had unfolded. "Maybe now you'll know better than to fall in love with a man who has only ever loved money," Alina smirked and shook her head as she studied Lawrence with absolute disgust.

"Why are you arresting him?" Mike shouted as he approached the police car. "What are you doing? Do you have any idea who my father is?"

"I know exactly who he is," Mitchell replied as he turned to look at Mike. His shoulders spread and his chest puffed out as he waited to see if Mike was going to become violent. "Your father is under arrest for murder," he said sternly. "The murder of Simon Carter."

"What?" Mike gasped his eyes wide. "Dad?" he peered into the police car, but Lawrence refused to look at him. "Dad! Tell him it's not true," he demanded. "You would never hurt Simon. You wouldn't, would you?" he pleaded, and despite the fact that he was a grown man it sounded as if he was begging his father as a child would. "You didn't do this, did you?" he murmured as Charlene walked up behind him and gently placed a hand on his back.

"Mike, let him be," she coaxed him.

"No," he cried out in a strangled voice. "I want him to tell me the truth! I know he was sleeping with Jane, and I know that was bad, but murder, Dad? Did you really kill your own son?"

Lawrence kept his head turned away from his only remaining son. His nieces were gasping and whispering to one another as well as to their spouses. It was obvious that none of them had ever expected that Lawrence could be capable of something like this. Mitchell closed the door to the police car and looked at the group of people gathered together.

"They're going to take him down to the station. If any of you know his lawyer, it would be best that you contact him." They all watched as Lawrence was driven away in the police car, leaving Mitchell standing in the parking lot.

Mike hung his head as Charlene slid her arm fully around his waist. She held tightly to him as she guided him inside.

"I can't believe he did this," Mike said quietly as he looked up at his cousins and uncle. "I still just can't believe it."

"I can," Alina muttered as she followed them inside. "A man who only respects money doesn't know the value of his own child."

Jane remained outside, her hands shifting from her pockets to being clasped behind her back, as if she had no idea what to do with them. She looked so sad with her mascara streaked across her cheeks, her eyes puffy from crying, and her expression dazed with shock.

"I never thought he would kill him," Jane whispered more to herself than anyone else. "How could I have been so foolish?"

"Are you okay, Jane?" Vicky asked as she walked towards her. Aunt Ida was talking quietly to Mitchell. Vicky had sympathy for Jane even though she had been having an affair with Lawrence, she had still lost the man who actually loved her.

"It was my fault," Jane whispered, her shoulders trembling with tears that had not fallen. "Lawrence convinced me that Simon didn't really love me. He said he was just marrying for looks, that Simon had insisted on a pre-nuptial to make sure I wouldn't get anything. He warned me that in ten years Simon would be trading me in for a younger model, just like Lawrence had his first wife. I didn't believe him at first, I loved Simon so much, but the more he told me these things, the more I guess, I just couldn't imagine someone like Simon actually being in love with me. I can't believe I believed Lawrence," she groaned and closed her eyes.

"Now, you know that what Lawrence said was not true," Vicky said quietly as she reached out to gently touch the woman's shoulder. "Simon did love you, and he wanted you to have everything he could offer you. But it was not your fault that he died. That was Lawrence's choice to commit such a horrible act."

"Maybe," Jane sniffled as she looked away from Vicky. "But it doesn't really change anything, does it?" she asked as she looked back at Vicky wistfully. "Simon's still gone. One minute we're getting ready for the future, the next... there's no future at all."

"No, it doesn't change that," Vicky admitted as she frowned. Jane's words made her think of her own conversation with Mitchell.

"Thanks for being so understanding, Vicky," Jane said quietly. "I'm so very sorry that Simon is dead, but I'm glad to be walking away from this family, if anyone could even call it that."

Vicky arched her brow at that as she tended to agree with that comment. "I used to be so envious of the Carters," Jane admitted in a murmur. "I grew up in a very poor home and all I ever dreamed of was ending up in one of those huge houses, never wanting for anything. But now," she laughed bitterly as she shook her head. "All I want is that tiny little house, and the people who actually cared about me. I just want to go home."

Vicky gave Jane's shoulder a light squeeze. "I'll arrange a cab for you," she said softly. "I think it's time you had some peace."

Jane gasped back a sob and nodded.

As Vicky turned to walk back into the inn, Mitchell jogged up the steps after her. He caught up with her just beside the front door.

"Vicky, wait," Mitchell said gently as he caught her wrist with his hand. "Can we talk for a minute?" he asked and met her eyes. She could tell from the determination in them that he wasn't going to take no for an answer. She had been trying to avoid this conversation for some time, but now it had to happen. "The other night," Mitchell continued when she didn't answer, "I know we both said some things that might not have been said if I hadn't been pressuring you."

"You weren't really pressuring me," Vicky countered as she searched his gaze. "It's just..."

"You don't owe me an explanation," Mitchell insisted as he let his hand drift from her wrist and close around hers. "I just jumped the gun, I see that now. It wasn't right for me to just assume that you would want the same things I did."

"Maybe not," Vicky bit into her bottom lip and glanced away shyly. She knew what she wanted to say, she just wasn't sure how to say it. His hand around hers was so comforting that she could barely recall why she had been so determined to avoid him. "Or maybe, I just wasn't ready to think about it," Vicky suggested and looked back up at him. "Sometimes I think we have forever, but forever often turns out to be a lot shorter than you expect."

"What do you mean?" Mitchell asked with a mixture of curiosity and concern.

"Like Jane," Vicky tilted her head towards the woman who was waiting for a cab to drive her home. She was sitting alone on a bench near the driveway.

"Wait, what could you have in common with a woman who was sleeping with her fiancé's father?" Mitchell asked with growing confusion.

"Not that part," Vicky shook her head, her hair tumbling down towards her eyes as she turned back to him again. "I mean, I doubt that she ever imagined she wouldn't have the chance to marry Simon. Before I knew everything that was going on behind the scenes, my heart broke for her. When I found Simon's body all I could think was that Jane would never have the chance to share that special moment with him."

"Oh," he breathed out as he stroked the back of her hand with his thumb. "I can understand what you mean. I guess working the job that I do, I think about that a little more often than other people do."

"I can see why," Vicky said softly. "Then today when Lawrence locked me in that shed, the very idea of me not having the chance to set things straight with you, it terrified me. I never, ever, want you to think that you're anything less than incredibly valuable to me."

"There's nothing to set straight," he assured her and stared into her eyes compassionately. "I was expecting too much."

"Or maybe I was just not expecting enough," Vicky countered as she slipped closer to him. She wrapped an arm around his waist and laid her head against his chest. He tensed for a moment as if he might not allow the connection, then his free hand drifted down over the back of her head and across her back. "When I said I wasn't ready for marriage and kids, that didn't mean that I didn't want those things with you," she murmured. "When I picture my future, you're the only man I see in it."

"Vicky, that's all I need to hear," he whispered and kissed the top of her head. "Whatever you decide, whenever you decide it, we'll take things at your pace."

"All I want right now is to know that your arms will always be around me," Vicky sighed as she relaxed in his embrace.

"They will be. That's something that you can always count on," he murmured beside her ear. Vicky melted into his arms, so glad to have him to comfort her after such a harrowing day. Even though she had no phone, she had no way to reach him, he had managed to come to her rescue, as he always did.

As Vicky pulled away from him to go into the inn and call the cab for Jane she felt a renewed sense of hope for the future. In the past she had always avoided looking too far into the future, because she wasn't sure how she hoped it would unfold. But now she knew one thing for sure, she wanted Mitchell to be part of it.

The End

More Cozy Mysteries by Cindy Bell

Heavenly Highland Inn Cozy Mystery Series

Murdering the Roses

Dead in the Daisies

Killing the Carnations

Bekki the Beautician Cozy Mystery Series

Hairspray and Homicide

A Dyed Blonde and a Dead Body

Mascara and Murder

Pageant and Poison

Conditioner and a Corpse

Makeup, Mistletoe and Murder

Blush, a Bride and a Body

Printed in Great Britain
by Amazon